OTHER BOOKS

Addison Holmes Mystery Series

Whiskey Rebellion
Whiskey Sour
Whiskey For Breakfast
Whiskey, You're The Devil
Whiskey on the Rocks
Whiskey Tango Foxtrot
Whiskey and Gunpowder

JJ Graves Mystery Series

Dirty Little Secrets
A Dirty Shame
Dirty Rotten Scoundrel
Down and Dirty
Dirty Deeds
Dirty Laundry
Dirty Money
A Dirty Job

The Harley and Davidson Mystery Series

The Farmer's Slaughter
A Tisket a Casket
I Saw Mommy Killing Santa Claus
Get Your Murder Running
Deceased and Desist
Malice In Wonderland
Tequila Mockingbird
Gone With the Sin

The MacKenzies of Montana

Dane's Return
Thomas's Vow
Riley's Sanctuary
Cooper's Promise
Grant's Christmas Wish
The MacKenzies Boxset

MacKenzie Security Series

Seduction and Sapphires
Shadows and Silk
Secrets and Satin
Sins and Scarlet Lace
Sizzle
Crave
Trouble Maker
Scorch
MacKenzie Security Omnibus 1
MacKenzie Security Omnibus 2

WHISKEY ON THE ROCKS

AN ADDISON HOLMES SHORT

LILIANA HART

WHISKEY ON THE ROCKS

An Addison Holmes Short

By

New York Times bestselling author

Liliana Hart

DEDICATION

For Scott,

Thanks for being my first reader. I love hearing you laugh.

PROLOGUE

FRIDAY

I'VE SEEN a lot of male genitalia in my life.

Okay, maybe not a lot. But I've seen a few in real life, and I might have seen one or two in a dirty movie Nick and I rented a few months back. I wasn't impressed by the movie genitalia. All I could think was that those poor girls must get a lot of urinary tract infections.

And if I'm being honest, male genitalia is not the most attractive thing on the planet, even when it belongs to someone like Nick, who has very impressive attributes and knows just what to do with them. I've always thought male dangly bits looked something along the lines of a forlorn Snuffleupagus—a little sad, with a droopy trunk, and tufts of hair sprouting every which way.

My name is Addison Holmes, and there's a reason genitalia is at the forefront of my mind. I'm a private investigator at the McClean Detective Agency. By the grace of God and hot fudge sundaes, I'd somehow managed to pass all portions of the exam that allowed me to carry the laminated license with my photo on it, as well as the pink-handled 9mm I kept in my Kate Spade handbag. I'd bought the Glock and the handbag out of the trunk of Louis Bergman's Cadillac when I'd gone home to Whiskey Bayou for the holidays. He'd been running a two-for-one special.

A fat lot of good the handbag and Glock were doing me now though. It would look a little foolish to be carrying an almost-genuine Kate Spade around a nudist colony, and carrying concealed wasn't really an option. The best I could do was hide my Glock under a towel in the beach bag I carried.

I was uncomfortable enough standing on the pier in the buff with Rosemarie and Aunt Scarlet at my side. A three-thousand-dollar camera hung around my neck, leaving a very interesting tan line down the center of each of my boobs from the strap. I'd been pretending to take pictures of seagulls for the last fifteen minutes, when in fact, I was trying to take pictures of Elmer Hughes, a man whose Snuffleupagus was approximately a hundred years old and looked like it suffered from elephantiasis.

"Lord, would you look at the testicles on that man," Aunt Scarlet said. "They're the size of oranges. How do you think he keeps from sitting on them?"

"You think he's had implants?" Rosemarie asked.

"I've heard plastic surgeons down here make a killing on senior citizens. People get to a certain age and then want to discover the fountain of youth."

"And testicular implants are supposed to make you look younger?" I asked skeptically, trying to zoom in on Elmer.

"Everything droops when you get to be my age," Scarlet said. "We associate tight and firm with youthfulness. Instead of getting the implants, he should've given those puppies a facelift. They almost hang all the way to his knees."

Elmer was down on the beach under one of the umbrellas, sunning on a lounger top side up, making sure his oranges got plenty of sun. I could barely get a decent shot of the tattoo on his arm, and even with the full zoom and focus of the camera, it was still difficult to make out. Age hadn't been kind to Elmer Hughes.

"I thought about getting my lady parts tightened up a bit," Scarlet continued. "They call it vaginal rejuvenation, if you can believe that. I haven't had anything rejuvenating down there since the time I walked through Wally Pinkerton's yard and all the sprinklers came on."

"Umm," I said, for lack of anything better.

"I was going to get rejuvenated because a couple of years ago I thought I might be getting some action, and I wanted everything to look as if it just came out of the factory. But the fellow up and died on me before we could get all hot and bothered. Take my advice, Addison. Never let a man die when they're lying on top of you. Thank God he was wearing one of those medic alert buttons around his neck, because I never would've been able to push him off to reach the phone."

I was in a complete state of Zen. Or it could have been the Xanax I'd taken with my mojito at lunch. There was no other way to survive being naked with two people I had no desire to be naked with, or to listen to the conversation we were currently having without it.

"It's probably best you opted out of the surgery," Rosemarie said. "Sharon Osbourne said it was excruciating."

"Ehh, I don't have much feeling left down there anyway," Scarlet said with a shrug. "I've stopped holding out hope."

"You've just got to wait for a man who's big enough to make things seem not so loosey-goosey down there."

Since Scarlet had just celebrated her ninetieth, I was thinking finding that particular man might be a challenge.

"I'm going to have to get closer," I said, hoping this would distract them from the conversation.

"Look," Rosemarie said. "Those loungers right next to him just came open. Let's get them before someone else does. You should be able to take plenty of pictures from that angle."

I sighed and let go of the camera so it hung around my neck. I wanted to say there was something freeing about standing completely naked on the pier, the wind tousling my hair and the sun beating down on my bare skin, but I'd be lying. I pretty much felt just like I had during middle school—awkward posture due to not knowing what to do with my body, awkward hair that frizzed in humidity no matter how much I straightened it, and awkward friends that pretty much guaranteed a lot of time standing next to the punch bowl at school dances.

I'd had my nether regions freshly waxed for this occasion and my body was still in pretty good shape from when I'd passed the physical fitness portion of my P.I. exam. I maintained the physique by doing hot yoga one day a week and occasionally watching a Jillian Michaels DVD from the couch. She scared the crap out of me. My butt cheeks clenched every time she screamed at someone that unless they were going to puke, faint, or die then they should keep going. My butt was really starting to look good.

"I still don't understand how you could recognize that tattoo," I said to Scarlet. "It's so wrinkled and distorted it's nearly impossible to make out."

"Some things you don't forget," she said sagely. "The Savannah bank robbery of '45 and a Latin lover named Mario are the two things that stick with me the most. Whew, was your Uncle Stan steamed about Mario. But once I explained he was Spanish royalty and it was an honor to be asked to sleep with him, Stan calmed right down." She looked confused for a minute and slapped her hand on top of her head to keep her hat from blowing away. "May he rest in peace."

Rosemarie and I stared at Scarlet with horrified fascination, and I did a half-assed sign of the cross along with Rosemarie and Scarlet at the mention of Uncle Stanley's untimely demise. I was mostly Methodist, so I was never really sure if I was crossing myself correctly, but no one had made devil horn signs at me or doused me with holy water yet, so I figured I was in the clear.

We made our way back to the stairs that led down to the beach and I dug my flip-flops out of my bag so the sand wouldn't burn my feet. I thought I looked like an idiot wearing nothing but a camera and flip-flops, but to those at the Hidden Sunrise Naturist Community, I looked like I belonged.

We spread our towels out on the loungers, adjusted the umbrellas so we were protected from direct sunlight, and got comfortable. I set the camera on the little table next to the loungers and pointed it at Elmer, who seemed to be snoozing peacefully on the lounger a few feet away.

The problem with the camera was that it made noise when pictures were taken, and I didn't know how sound of a sleeper Elmer was. So I used my second best option and pulled out my iPhone.

The beach waiter came up and took our drink orders, and I sighed, frustrated, because I couldn't get a clear shot of the tattoo on Elmer's arm with my phone. I had to have the tattoo. It was the only documented proof the FBI had of the Romeo Bandit, a.k.a., Elmer Hughes.

I watched Elmer for ten more minutes and contemplated my choices while I sipped on a Sex on the Beach. Rosemarie was reading a book two loungers over, and Aunt Scarlet had gotten bored and was building a sand castle, wearing nothing but a big hat and a lot of sand she was probably going to regret getting up close and personal with later.

"Don't forget the sunscreen, Aunt Scarlet," I called out a little too loud, watching Elmer closely to see if he stirred. Nope. He was down for the count. It was now or never.

I took another fortifying sip of my drink, put the camera strap around my neck and got on all fours in the hot sand. I might have muttered an expletive or two, having not thought through the fact that it would feel like dipping my hands and knees in molten glass.

I tried not to think about what I looked like from behind. And then I did think about it and grabbed the towel off my lounger, draping it across my backside like a tablecloth. I slowly crawled on hands and knees until I was inches away from Elmer Hughes.

My heart was pounding in my chest and I was covered with sweat and sand, neither of my favorite things. I realized I had a slight buzz and the Xanax must have worn off because I was feeling a whole lot of anxiety all of a sudden.

Elmer let out a soft snore and I squeaked. His arm

was limp and his hands were gnarled with age. He wore a pinky ring with a small ruby in the center. The tattoo was wrinkled and the ink had faded over the years, but now that I was up close, I could see it clearly. A thorny vine and rosary beads were twined around a naked woman that had more curves than Kim Kardashian. The vine and the rosary beads ended at the top of his hand where the rose had started to bloom.

I could see how in its heyday the tattoo might have been an interesting conversation piece, but the inked woman was now wizened with age and arm hair, and it looked vaguely as if she were shooting the rosary out of her vagina. But Aunt Scarlet had recognized it, and that was all that mattered.

I brought the camera up and took a couple of quick shots, and then I bit my lip as I debated whether or not to stretch his skin out a little and get a more complete picture. I finally decided that was the alcohol talking and probably not the best decision, and then I realized the alcohol had been giving me directions through this whole debacle because what I was doing definitely wasn't using my best judgment.

I found this out the hard way when I turned to crawl back to my own lounger and my towel got stuck under my knee, pulling it completely off and leaving me bare-assed with my lady bits flapping in the breeze.

"Yikes," a male voice said behind me.

I scrambled to cover my rear with the towel and

turned my head in time to catch Elmer Hughes's horrified stare.

"Jesus God," he wheezed, clutching his chest. "I thought I was having a flashback from the seventies. Those things looked a lot different then. That's nothing like '70s bush. You've got a nice landscaper."

I turned fifty shades of red and scrambled to make sure I was completely covered with the towel. And then I noticed his gaze had shifted to the camera in my hand.

"I can explain," I said.

CHAPTER ONE

It wouldn't be the South if there weren't proverbial skeletons in everyone's closets.

We certainly had our fair share in my family, and I knew other families had their fair share too, because we still talked about them in the checkout line at the Piggly Wiggly or with the cashier at Dairy Queen while waiting on an ice cream sundae.

It was January and dreary and cold in Whiskey Bayou, Georgia. I'd temporarily moved back home due to the fact that my boyfriend, Nick Dempsey, had proposed and I'd had a moment of panic where I saw myself the last time I'd been about to get married— big poofy white dress and cake for two hundred— only to catch my fiancé boffing my archenemy in our honeymoon limo.

They say lightning doesn't strike the same place twice, but the proposal and subsequent panic attack were enough that I knew I needed some time and space to think about the proposal and being married to Nick for the rest of my life.

So I did what any girl does when unsure of the future. I moved back home with my mother. There are two problems with this. One: I worked in Savannah and the drive was a real bitch. And two: I was living at home with my mother.

Don't get me wrong. I love my mother dearly. And maybe we're more alike than I'm comfortable admitting. But living in the same house with her is enough to put me over the edge. Not to mention she's newly married and the walls are thin at Casa de Holmes.

Needless to say, I'd spent the last couple of weeks since the infamous proposal working as much as humanly possible so I wouldn't have to act like an adult and face my issues head-on. I had to admit, I was missing Nick. I'd gotten used to him. Which was really what marriage was all about—getting used to someone enough that you didn't want to murder them if you had to spend more than a few hours a day with them.

I was currently sprawled out on the leather couch in Kate's office, regretting the second cinnamon roll I'd just devoured and wondering how much Jillian Michaels butt clenching I'd have to do to make up the calories. My best friend, Kate McClean, owner of the McClean Detective Agency, sat in the chair just across from me.

That's when I heard the ruckus from down the hall. I was the daughter of a cop. And Kate was a former cop. So unless there was active gunfire neither of us were known to sweat the small stuff. Okay, maybe I sometimes sweated the small stuff, but it usually had to do with Black Friday specials and Louboutins being on sale. I was a seven, so my size always went fast.

"I'm here to see my niece and you can't stop me," a familiar voice—both fragile and four-star general— roared over me like a freight train. "I've got a .44 in here and I'm not afraid to use it. Better step out of my way, Elvira."

My eyes widened and I saw the pure fear on Kate's face at the thought of my Aunt Scarlet tangling with Lucy, the gatekeeper for the agency. Nobody made it past Lucy unless they were an employee or a client. I had my suspicions about Lucy. The two most prom-inent being that she'd worked for the CIA at some point or that she was a vampire—though I hadn't really figured out how she got around the whole sunlight issue.

We both shot up to a standing position and started running, but we went through the door at the same time and got stuck. It was then I noticed Lucy standing at the end of the hallway, her red lips pressed firmly together as she stood her ground. But Aunt Scarlet had worked as a spy for the OSS during World War II and she'd outlived five husbands, so nothing much intimidated her.

"Aunt Scarlet," I called out, shoving past Kate.

Aunt Scarlet was digging in her purse and pulling out a .44 revolver the size of a cannon. It was so heavy she couldn't lift it and she shot a hole in the floor between Lucy's feet.

I guess that was enough to stun Lucy because Scarlet pushed right by her and headed straight for us.

"I don't remember that gun having such a sensitive trigger," Scarlet said. "That sucker packs a punch. It was like getting kicked in the hot box by a mule."

I was afraid to ask what she meant by "hot box" but I'd gotten pretty good at interpreting Scarlet-speak over the course of my life. It had been three years since I'd last seen her, and the trauma of it all made it feel like yesterday. My mother was going to have kittens.

Scarlet was my father's aunt. Which meant she was my great-aunt. And she was our skeleton in the closet. She'd grown up as a Holmes in Whiskey Bayou during the Great Depression, and the family gossip was that she'd been shipped off to Paris by her father because she'd been having affairs with a couple of married men and they'd challenged each other to a duel, agreeing that the winner would get to keep Scarlet to himself.

Apparently Scarlet had been quite a looker in her day —a dead ringer for Ava Gardner, some people said— but she'd been rather loose with her virtue. Scarlet had never seemed to mind. When I was twelve, she'd told me it was better to be loose with your virtue than loose with your bank account. If I'd listened to

Scarlet I'd probably be a lot more sexed up and a lot richer.

The days of Ava Gardner had long passed, and Scarlet now looked like Hannibal Lecter had put all of her bones in a skin bag and shaken them up so nothing quite fit together. She got around better than she should have for someone her age, and she attributed it to the fact that she'd smoked unfiltered cigarettes when she was younger and her insides were pickled from highballs.

The black wool coat she wore swallowed her whole and she'd left it unbuttoned, displaying a leopard-print velour jogging suit beneath. She wore white tennis shoes that were so bright they hurt to look at and a magenta scarf was wrapped around her neck. Her hair was a shock of white that had been permed within an inch of its life and shellacked with such success that not even the misty rain and frigid winter wind had budged it. She topped off the look with the signature bright red lipstick I'd never seen her without.

"I smell cinnamon rolls," she said, shoving her gun back in her handbag and brushing past me and Kate. "I didn't get breakfast."

Scarlet followed her nose into Kate's office and shrugged out of her coat, handing it to Kate to hang up. She left the scarf around her neck.

"Do you have a permit for that gun, Scarlet?" Kate asked.

"Darling, I don't need a permit. I was in the OSS. I have a pass."

"They don't hand out passes to carry weapons because you slept with Nazis seventy years ago."

"I've always liked you, Kate," Scarlet said with a smile. "Let me give you some advice. Germans are terrible in bed. Avoid them at all costs. But if you want to get them to talk, just stick your finger straight up their butthole. Works every time."

Scarlet looked around the room and wandered to Kate's desk, picking up the candy dish of Hershey's Kisses and sticking the entire thing into her purse.

"I'm married," Kate said dryly. "He's Scottish."

"Well, maybe you can do better next time, dearie. I enjoyed my fourth husband immensely."

Scarlet poured herself a cup of coffee and helped herself to one of the cinnamon rolls before sitting in the chair Kate normally occupied during meetings.

"Sit, girls. Time is of the essence here. I could die tomorrow."

I shrugged and freshened my coffee and got a new cup for Kate as well. Kate and I had been friends forever, but sometimes I was a trial. And that included stray family members that had popped in and out of my life through the years.

"Does Mom know you're in town?" I asked, taking my usual spot on the sofa next to Kate.

"Heavens no. And we're going to keep this our little

secret. Your mother is always trying to steal my thunder. There can only be one eccentric in a family and until I die that's me."

Though Scarlet had been married five times, she'd stopped changing her name after her second husband because she hated the lines at the social security office. She'd said she was born Scarlet Holmes and that's how she wanted to die.

"I thought you were living on one of those cruise ships," Kate said.

Scarlet waved the statement away and took a bite of the cinnamon roll. She was a Holmes all right. I got that same look on my face whenever eating sweets or having an orgasm.

"That ended after Thanksgiving. I think the captain was drugging me and sneaking into my room at night to fondle me. I woke up every morning with a horrible hangover and no underwear. He tried to tell me it was because I was drinking too much and leaving my underpants on the craps table for good luck, but that's ridiculous. I don't even play craps. Everyone knows that roulette is my game."

A horrible thought struck me and I blurted out, "Are you moving back to Whiskey Bayou?"

"Hell no," she said, appalled. "Lord, I hate that place. Though I like to go and visit the cemetery because I know everyone buried there. It's a lot easier to talk to people when they don't have the capability of talking back."

She let out a gentle belch and then leaned back and propped her sneakered feet on the table.

"After the cruise ship I found a little resort place in Florida. It's always warm and it's right on the water. I can't wait to get back. This cold is terrible on my bones. Can't even feel my nipples. I smashed one of them in the car door and didn't even notice."

"You drove here?" I asked, unsuccessful at keeping the terror out of my voice.

"You bet. Just bought a brand new Hummer. It's a real beaut. You don't even notice when you run over things."

"Christ," Kate said under her breath.

"How long are you staying?" I asked.

"That's what I'm trying to explain. We need to get back there lickety-split."

"We?" Kate and I said together.

"You girls don't have the sense that God gave a goose. I'm trying to tell you something important here. I've found a murderer!"

CHAPTER TWO

YOU MIGHT THINK one would get excited or concerned over Scarlet's news. But the truth was, Scarlet had a tendency to bend the truth on occasion. She also had the tendency to steal things that caught her eye, and she'd once gotten caught using a blow dart gun when the Jehovah's Witnesses wouldn't leave her alone.

"You girls are very calm and have excellent poker faces," she said, nodding. "The OSS could've used you."

I was personally glad to hear this, because I'd been working on my poker face. Before I'd started working for Kate, pretty much everything I thought was broadcast on my face for the world to see.

"We've dealt with our fair share of murderers," Kate said diplomatically. "Did you witness the murder?"

"I sure as heck did," she said.

This caught me by surprise. Either she was hallucinating and making up a heck of a story or she'd really witnessed a murder. Her answer had been definitive.

"That no-good bastard Elmer Hughes is a cold-blooded killer. And he's my neighbor to boot. Nearly scared me to death when I saw him eating alone in one of the restaurants at the resort. I couldn't even finish my crème brulee."

She must've been terrified. Not much came between a Holmes and dessert.

Scarlet's eyes narrowed to beady slits and she tapped her crimson nails on the arm of the chair. "I'm not a coward. They didn't call me Bouncing Betty during the war for nothing. So I walked right up and asked if he'd like some company. He didn't remember me. The bastard. I admit I've changed a little since the last time we saw each other, but I haven't changed *that* much."

"When was the last time you saw him?" Kate asked.

"When I was seventeen."

Kate and I both stayed silent. I'd seen pictures of Scarlet at seventeen. The only thing that looked even remotely the same from those days was the color of her eyes—and even that had faded a bit.

"Seventeen?" Kate asked. "This isn't a current murder?"

"Don't be so impatient, girl. I'm getting to that. There's no statute of limitations for murder, right?"

"Right," Kate said. "Sorry, keep going."

"He went by Frank back when I knew him, and Lord, was he a handsome devil. Charming too. He had me wrapped right around his little finger."

"Did he break your heart? Is that the real reason Grandpa Holmes shipped you off to Paris?" I asked curiously.

In secret, I kind of wanted to be like Scarlet, but I was already in my thirties and certain parts of my body weren't as high up as they used to be. I wasn't holding out hope for spying for our country or having mad affairs with handsome foreigners. Though the more I thought about it, I *was* spying for the McClean Detective Agency, and I was having a mad affair with a hot Irish detective, and I'd almost had a mad affair with a super-hot Native American FBI agent. I was cultural as shit. And maybe I was more like Aunt Scarlet than I knew.

"Hell, no," she said. "I wanted to go to Paris. Men are nothing but trouble. You sleep with them and all of a sudden they think they own you. And then they do stupid things like shoot each other. Here's more free advice. Penises mostly all look and function the same. Ride it until it's dead and then move on."

I sighed and thought I might need a third cinnamon roll to get through this conversation.

"Getting back to Elmer—or Frank—whoever he is…" Kate said.

"Like I was saying, Frank charmed the pants right off

of me. We only had one night together, but it's still one of my top five sexual experiences. He was an animal. A real beast. Lordy, it's getting hot in here," she said, unzipping her leopard-print jacket.

"What happened? Did he sneak out on you in the middle of the night?" I asked, getting a little worked up myself. I hadn't had sex in three weeks.

"Of course not," she said. "No man has ever snuck out on me in the middle of the night."

Scarlet brought her feet down from the table and leaned forward, staring at both of us intently. I couldn't help but lean forward myself, waiting for whatever was coming with anticipation.

"The next morning I went to my job as a teller at the bank, and about ten minutes after we opened we were held up at gunpoint. He was masked, but there was something about the way he moved that seemed familiar to me. The hips don't lie, you know. Somebody famous once said that," she said, nodding with great wisdom. "Frank waltzed right up and handed me a long-stemmed rose while he pointed the gun at my face and demanded that I put money in the bag."

"Holy shit," I said, my mouth hanging open.

"Yep. That about sums up my reaction too. And then he shot my friend Susan right in the face."

CHAPTER THREE

"So you're saying the Elmer you walked up to in the restaurant is Frank the bank robber?" Kate asked.

Scarlet nodded. "They called him the Romeo Bandit. He always seduced a female that worked at the bank and then gave them a red rose as a parting gift when he robbed them."

"They never caught him?" Kate asked.

"Never," Scarlet said. "At the time, he was one of the most wanted men in America. When he robbed the bank in Whiskey Bayou he was already a pro and had been at it for several years. He'd robbed more than twenty banks all over the country and killed more than a dozen people. I never suspected a thing."

"He didn't ask questions about the set-up of the bank when you were out together?" Kate asked.

Scarlet laughed and her rheumy eyes brightened, showing a glint of wickedness. "Honey, we didn't go out together. I never had a chance," she said, shaking her head. "To this day, I've never seen a man as handsome as he was. Maybe Sean Connery in his prime comes close, but that still doesn't do him justice. He was one of those men that just oozed raw sex appeal. And not to toot my own horn, but I'd been known to have my fair share of sex appeal too. I might have only been seventeen, but when I looked at him I felt like the most worldly of women."

She sighed and I knew exactly how she felt. That's how I'd reacted the first time I met Nick.

"It was a Tuesday just before close, and I was drawn to him the moment he walked through the doors of the bank. He came right up to me and asked to open a new account. Lord, Susan was peeved that he never looked twice at her. She told me straight to my face that I exuded trampiness and that's why men always approached me first.

"Let me tell you, I looked like a lady. And I *was* a lady outside the bedroom," she said, waggling her eyebrows. "That's the trick, girls. Men are drawn to confident women who own their looks and sex appeal. And it drives them crazy when they see properness on the outside and can only imagine what might be unleashed in the bedroom. I'm giving you girls all this free advice because I love you like family."

"I am family, Aunt Scarlet," I said.

"Then you're especially lucky I'm not charging you.

Family is a pain in the ass. But you remind me a little of me, so I've always been partial to you."

"Thank you. I think."

"Like I said, he went by the name Frank in those days. Frank DeCosta. And he had proper identification and everything. He deposited two hundred dollars and asked if I was free after closing for coffee. I told him I was available for dinner. He winked at me, and then left the bank. I wondered if I'd misplayed my hand, but when I walked out of the bank that night he was leaning against his car. He had a bottle of champagne chilling in the backseat and a dozen red roses."

"Smooth," I said, admiring the play. They didn't make men like they used to.

"Oh, yes. And if I'd been thinking with the brain in my head instead of my loins I would've realized he'd had to prepare all of that before he came into the bank. There was no place close by to get roses or champagne. It was Whiskey Bayou and it was 1943. We weren't known for our sophistication and class."

"Nothing much has changed," I told her.

"It was pure romance," she said. "We drove around until we found a secluded area, and then we drank the champagne and talked. God, he was easy to talk to. Susan had called me a tramp, but I knew good and well what I was. I was a young woman looking for any way possible to escape my father and get the hell out of Whiskey Bayou. And the only way to do that was to find a man with plenty of money to take me out of there."

"An admirable goal," I said. I understood the need to escape Whiskey Bayou. I'd felt the urge to run screaming out of town since grade school, but I guess my goals hadn't been as lofty as Scarlet's. I'd never thought of trying to marry my way out.

"I tell you," Scarlet said. "The Lord works in mysterious ways. If Frank hadn't robbed me that day and made me lose my job, I never would have been at loose ends and seduced Roger Greene when I went to his law office to apply for secretarial work. And if I hadn't gotten the job as Roger's secretary, I never would've met Dean Walker when I went to the distillery to order bottles of whiskey for Roger to send to his best clients. Dean had more money than Croesus, but he didn't know jack squat about love-making. Never in my life have I met a man that didn't know a clitoris from an elbow."

Scarlet shook her head in pure disgust. "And if I hadn't taken those men to my bed, they never would've tried to kill each other to win me over and I never would've gotten sent to Paris, where I met my dear first husband, Pierre, who *did* happen to know an elbow from a clitoris. Of course, he was a spy and dragged me into the whole thing by accident. But it turned out I was pretty good at being a spy, and Pierre got shot while on assignment and I ended up with all his money, so things turned out okay."

"Yes, I can see how that was all the Lord's work," Kate said dryly.

"Anyway, back to Frank. We finished our champagne, and drunk on hormones and expensive champagne, we went back to my place, where he showed great ingenuity by climbing up the side of the house to sneak into my bedroom window. For the next eight hours we didn't leave that bed. And we didn't do any sleeping either, if you catch my drift. He left just before the sun came up, and I had to be at the bank at eight o'clock to open up."

I decided to be brave and speak up. "I still don't understand how you're so sure this Elmer guy you met at your retirement village is the Romeo Bandit. It's been more than seventy years. I'm sure he looks very…different," I said, thinking that if Elmer had changed as much as Scarlet had he was probably virtually unrecognizable.

"That's what I'm saying. There are some things that you can't erase. And one of those is tattoos. It's how I knew for sure it was him when he robbed the bank. Frank had a tattoo that covered the whole bottom half of his arm. Tattoos in those days weren't common, especially in visible locations. Especially something as crude as a naked woman. She was a voluptuous thing with dark hair, and I didn't even know he had it until I got him naked and tied to the bed."

My eyebrows rose and Kate had chosen that unfortunate time to take a sip of coffee. I pounded her on the back a couple of times until she waved me off.

"So what you're saying is Elmer has the same tattoo as Frank?" Kate asked after she'd gotten herself under control. "Couldn't it be possible that someone else could have the same tattoo?"

"I doubt it," Scarlet said. "It's very distinct. When I asked him about the tattoo he told me the woman was his wife. She'd died in childbirth a couple of years before and it was his memorial to her. He'd given her a long-stemmed red rose on their first date and he laid one on her casket after she died. He had the rose twined around her body in the tattoo, along with a rosary, so that she might rest in peace."

"That's sad," I said.

"Yep, I'm a real romantic at heart, so that story was a little bit of a buzzkill. I almost untied him and suggested we go out for dinner after all, but he turned things around pretty quick. It turns out he didn't even need his hands to get the job done. That's talent right there."

Kate and I both nodded in agreement. That was indeed a talent.

"Frank told me that his wife always called him her Romeo. And the word Romeo was written in fancy script right between his wife's legs. Not his real wife," she clarified. "The tattoo of the wife."

"Gotcha," I said.

"Do you know what this means?" Scarlet asked. "After more than seventy years, I've caught the Romeo Bandit. Do you think there's a reward?"

CHAPTER FOUR

IT TURNED out there *was* a reward. A really, really big one. And I was suddenly a lot more interested in the Romeo Bandit's capture. If, in fact, Elmer was the Romeo Bandit. First we had to prove it.

Kate got her laptop from her desk and set it up on the coffee table. "What's Elmer's full alias?" she asked Scarlet.

"Elmer Hughes. He lives in Villa one twenty-seven—three down from mine. He walked me to my door after I asked if I could join him that evening, and he was quite the gentleman. You know what that means?" Scarlet asked with a snort.

"What?" I said curiously.

"It means his plumbing doesn't work anymore. That thing is useless as a monkey with a meat grinder. He didn't even try to kiss me goodnight."

"Uhh…" I said, for lack of anything better.

"Elmer Hughes," Kate said, breaking in. "Age ninety-two. Permanent residence listed as the Hidden Sunrise Naturist Community."

"Naturist. What's that? Like a tree-hugging retirement village?" I asked.

"It's a nudist colony," Kate said wryly.

I closed my eyes and shook my head from side to side, trying to clear the images from my mind. "Sweet Jesus," I muttered.

"Before we go on here," Kate said. "Are you officially hiring this agency to help identify and capture the Romeo Bandit?"

That's what I loved about Kate. She was all business, and she would charge her own mother for services. Though knowing the relationship between Kate and her mother, that probably wasn't the best example. She'd probably charge her double.

"You can have two percent of the finder's fee," Scarlet said, her eyes narrowing as she gave Kate the stink eye.

"Ten percent plus expenses," Kate countered. "If it turns out Elmer isn't the Romeo Bandit, you just cover the expenses. I'm giving you a discount. This is an exclusive agency. We're the best and we're expensive. I can put Addison undercover, and we'll have this solved in the next forty-eight hours."

"Hold on just a minute," I said, looking back and forth between Kate and Scarlet. "You're going to put me undercover at a nudist colony? Have you lost your damned mind?" Then I turned to Kate and hissed under my breath. "I don't want to look at a bunch of naked old people. I'll need therapy. Not to mention I haven't waxed my bikini line since Nick proposed, and I've maybe had an extra hot fudge sundae or two to help me get through this trying time. Nobody wants to see me naked right now."

"You look great naked," Kate said, rolling her eyes. "I saw you naked two weeks ago when that spider dropped on your head while you were in the shower. Hell, everyone in the whole office saw you naked and you didn't have any complaints then."

"That's hardly the same thing," I said primly. "This would be on purpose."

"You can go this afternoon and get a bikini wax. Put it on your expense report."

I narrowed my eyes and tightened my lips. This was war. "Oh, I'll put it on my expense report." Then I looked back at Scarlet. "The agency gets ten percent of the finder's fee and I get another ten percent for the indignity of it all. That still leaves a big chunk of the million-dollar reward for you."

Scarlet chewed on the inside of her cheek and stared me down like a gunslinger. "Yep, you're a Holmes all right. You've got yourself a deal. I'm due for a bikini wax myself. We can go together."

"Perfect," Kate said, her smile big and toothy. "Put them both on the expense report."

"I hate you," I mouthed.

She scratched her eye with her middle finger and then turned back to the computer. "There's nothing unusual that I'm seeing here. Elmer made his money from investments and retired about thirty years ago. He's been living off the residuals ever since."

"Get a grip, girl," Scarlet said. "It's not like you're going to type in his name in your little machine and an alarm's going to go off telling you Elmer's the Romeo Bandit. He's too smart for that, and he's been hiding under the radar for a long time."

"Can you find out anything in the FBI database?" I asked Kate.

Her mouth quirked and she said, "Not unless I want to go to jail. I don't have access to the FBI database."

"Oh, right. Sorry," I said. "I've kind of gotten used to working with Agent Savage."

Matt Savage had been playing a hell of a tug-of-war with my morals. I loved Nick, but there were some men that were just really good at muddying the waters. Savage had spent a good portion of the last year muddying my waters. And it didn't help matters any that he'd occasionally lent me his expertise and the use of his FBI contacts during a couple of my cases.

"I'm pretty sure Agent Savage could've lost his job a couple of times falling in with your schemes."

"I have no idea what you're talking about," I said primly.

"I'd like to meet this Agent Savage," Scarlet said.

"I've been thinking about becoming a cougar. He sounds exciting."

"He has his moments, but he's gay," I said, pulling out my cell phone to call him.

"That's a shame. Maybe I could turn him un-gay."

"I don't think it works that way," I told Scarlet as I put the phone to my ear.

"Savage," he said, and I immediately got the shivers.

"You know anything about the Romeo Bandit?" I asked by way of greeting.

"That's how you're going to say hello?" he asked. "No small talk? No quick bite to eat to catch up? We haven't seen each other in weeks. I thought we were friends."

"We are," I said, feeling a little guilty. I'd pretty much avoided all men for the last three weeks. And Savage was definitely a man.

"Good, let's have lunch."

I looked over at Scarlet and smiled. "My aunt is in town. I'd have to bring her with me."

There was silence on the other end and then a sigh. "Is this a lunch I'm probably going to regret?"

"Most definitely. But don't worry. I already told her you were gay."

Another few seconds of silence followed and I had a feeling Savage was weighing the pros and cons of friendship with me. I had that effect on a lot of people.

"Why do you need information on the Romeo Bandit?"

I wasn't about to take the chance of turning information over to the FBI and losing the reward. But at the same time I needed Savage's help. Knowledge was power.

"One of my old students is doing a report on the Romeo Bandit. There's not a lot of information in the database on him."

More silence. "That's the lamest excuse I've ever heard."

I sighed and flopped back on the couch.

"But because we're friends, let me look up the file and I'll tell you what I can. You're going to owe me big time though."

"Owe you how?" I asked.

"I'll think of something good."

His voice had lowered and I could hear the bad boy in it, just waiting to debauch a good girl like me. This was my problem with Savage. I was pretty sure there was a bad girl somewhere deep inside of me that wanted to be debauched. I had to stay away from Savage at all costs.

"Crap," I muttered under my breath.

"I heard that," he said.

I heard the clack of the keyboard as he typed and waited patiently for information. Mostly I was trying not to think about what the next forty-eight hours of my life were going to be like. If I was lucky, I might get hit by a plane before I had to see any old people naked.

"Okay, here we go," he said. And then he whistled long and low. "This is way before my time, but this guy was a badass. And I don't mean that in a complimentary way. One of the most successful bank robbers in history. He robbed a total of thirty-one banks between 1939 and 1945. He murdered twenty-two people in cold blood and left a long-stemmed red rose as a calling card. He was called the Romeo Bandit because he liked to seduce female employees of the bank sometime before he robbed them. Several of the women that admitted to sleeping with him mentioned an unusual tattoo on his arm."

"What happened after 1945?" I asked.

"He vanished off the face of the earth. There were no other robberies listed after that date. It could've had something to do with the war being over, or he could've died. No one knows. There's a million-dollar reward for his capture, though I'd have to say if he wasn't dead by now then he's probably pretty close to it."

"Hmm," I said. "Any idea about his true identity?"

"We have a list of the aliases he used over the six years he robbed banks. He never used the same name twice. We have several witness descriptions, and his appearance changed from time to time. Sometimes he had a mustache. Sometimes his hair was graying at the temples. They were all subtle differences. But judging from the statements of the women he seduced, they were literally so enamored with him that they didn't even think twice about his motives. He got away with hundreds of thousands of dollars in cash and gold."

"Maybe he just knew when to quit and retired," I said.

"Maybe," Savage said skeptically. "Anything else you need?"

"Do you have a description of the tattoo?"

"I've got several renderings taken from witness statements. They're all very similar. The women he seduced spent a lot of time looking at that tattoo."

"Can you send me a copy of one of the sketches?"

"I'll text it to you. Whatever you're up to, make sure you're careful," Savage warned. "This guy might be old, but he killed a lot of people."

"Right," I said, getting that squishy feeling in my stomach. "Maybe stay tuned in case I need bail money or need to go to the hospital."

"Ten-four. I'm going to pass on lunch today. I put on normal socks this morning because I haven't done laundry in a while. No one would believe I'm gay in normal socks."

"True," I agreed. "It's probably for the best anyway."

Savage was a rule breaker. Which was probably why we got along so well. Though I wasn't sure the FBI appreciated his rule breaking like I did…but he was the special agent in charge for the Savannah FBI satellite office, so he must've been doing something right.

I disconnected and looked at Scarlet. "Let's go catch the Romeo Bandit."

CHAPTER FIVE

FRIDAY...

BECAUSE MURPHY'S Law had conspired against me, I wasn't at all surprised to see Rosemarie Valentine at my door the next morning. I had no clue who Murphy was, but if we ever met face to face, I was going to punch him in the throat.

I'd spent the night back at my mother's house with an icepack on my nether regions in hopes the red puffiness from the waxing would go away before I had to take my clothes off at the Hidden Sunrise Naturist Community. Aunt Scarlet had changed her mind about the waxing since her skin was "as thin as paper" and she was afraid they'd rip it right off. She'd opted instead to have her pubic hair dyed hot pink.

So when I opened the door to Rosemarie, standing there with a bright and cheery smile without an umbrella to protect her from the drizzle, I barely even swore at all. I was almost expecting it.

"I'm playing hooky from school today," she said. "This weather is making me sad, and I've been auditioning students for *Evita* all week. I need a margarita in the worst way."

"It's eight o'clock in the morning," I said, moving back so she could step inside. We were both talking in hushed whispers because my mom and her husband were still in bed.

"I know. I was starting to have fantasies about tossing the kids down into the orchestra pit. Only the orchestra pit was full of snakes like in Indiana Jones."

Rosemarie was the choir teacher at the school I'd taught at before they'd canned me for improper behavior. We'd never been close while I was teaching, but since I started working at the detective agency, Rosemarie had become an unofficial mascot of sorts, as well as my friend.

She'd decided to go all out for a rainy winter day in Savannah—purple ski pants and a puffy matching jacket, turquoise fluffy earmuffs, and galoshes with pink flamingos on them. Rosemarie was on the plump side, so it was a lot of color to be greeted with first thing in the morning. Her normal blonde Farrah Fawcett curls were flattened and damp from the rain, and her cheeks were rosy from the cold.

It was winter in Savannah, which meant it was a breezy spring evening to every state north of here that had four seasons. But it was the only chance we got to pull out our Uggs and North Face attire, so we tried to take advantage.

"The snakes are probably a good sign for a break," I said. And then I heard the gentle squeak of the mattress and the headboard hitting the wall. They were sounds that couldn't be disguised.

"Wow, early risers, huh?" Rosemarie said.

"And late to bed," I told her. "Do you see these bags under my eyes? There's a reason I can only live with my mother for a short amount of time. I'm going to have to accept Nick's proposal just to get a decent night's sleep."

"So you're going to accept?" she asked, bouncing slightly on the balls of her feet.

"I'm not ready to talk about it. But I'm going to have to do something soon. It's been three weeks and the idea of sleeping in my car has more appeal than spending another night in this house. I'm waiting on my aunt to pick me up. She really needs to get here fast before my mother gets done and I have to look her in the face. I'm an adult. I know that she has sex, and I'm perfectly fine with that. But knowing and witnessing are two different things and I need at least twenty-four hours of sex distance before I can face her again."

"That's more than reasonable," Rosemarie said. She cocked her head to the side and listened intently as the mattress squeaks stayed steady. "But don't worry. She's going to be preoccupied for a while. They've got a nice rhythm going. They'll be at it for at least another hour. You know I once dated a man that was in his late fifties. There's something to be said for age. That man could go for hours without stopping."

"That doesn't sound so bad," I said, trying to be supportive.

"Are you kidding me?" she asked, appalled. "This body was not made for athletic sex of that magnitude. Don't get me wrong. I like to dig in and get dirty. But that was Olympic-level sex. After three hours of thrust time my lady parts were numb and I was nodding off right as he was getting going. I had to break things off. I wouldn't have survived."

Why did I always engage? I should've known better. But that's how friendship worked. One of you made a declaration, and if the other didn't engage in the conversation it just made you look like an asshole.

"Hey, they're revving things up in there," Rosemarie said. "They might be done sooner than we thought."

She was right. Mom and Vince had indeed picked up the pace, and accompanying moans sounded in harmony with the squeaky mattress. Listening to the crescendo was going to push me right over the edge, so I ushered us out the front door, along with my small travel suitcase.

We were now standing in the cold and drizzle, but sometimes escape was more important than hair and makeup. Granted, I could pretty much count on one finger the number of times anything was more important than hair or makeup. This was the South, and by God you'd better put on your best face and hair to shop at the Piggly Wiggly, otherwise you'd be the center of gossip for days. I was used to being the center of gossip, so it didn't bother me quite as bad as it once had to think Myrtle Strong was staring out her front window while I stood in the rain and let my perfectly straightened hair crinkle around my face.

A bright red Hummer pulled up in front of us, just in time, rolling right over one of the big planter urns my mother had set at the end of the sidewalk.

"Are you going on a trip?" Rosemarie asked. "And is that Scarlet Holmes? I thought she was an urban legend. Your family's been known to exaggerate a time or two."

I narrowed my eyes at Rosemarie. "All legends come from bits of the truth," I said primly. "And my family was one of the town's founders. Of course things are going to get blown out of proportion at times, but for the most part everything you hear is true."

"All right, all right. Don't get your panties in a twist. I'm just saying, Scarlet's infamous."

"For sleeping her way through the Nazi lines?" I asked skeptically.

"No," Rosemarie said, a confused look on her face. "Because she single-handedly stopped Francois Pinoit while she was working as a spy in France. I heard she bested him with nothing more than a paper-clip and a book of matches."

Okay, so maybe not everything about my family was mostly true. I'd never heard this story about Scarlet.

But Scarlet had a tendency to make up her own history.

"Scarlet and I are working a case," I said. "We've got to go to Florida for the weekend."

"Oh, that sounds way better than what I had in mind. Having margaritas in Florida sounds much better than having margaritas in Whiskey Bayou. I bet it's sunny and warm."

"Umm—" I said, trying to think of a delicate way of breaking it to Rosemarie that we were going to a nudist colony and she wasn't invited. "You see—"

I couldn't even say the words out loud. In my mind, going to a nudist colony wasn't even a reality in my world. I was going to need a lot of alcohol. And just in case, I'd stolen a handful of my mother's Xanax out of the medicine cabinet. She hardly ever used it anymore, since my sister Phoebe moved out. The prescription was a couple of years old, but I figured the expiration date was more of a guideline than an actual cutoff.

Scarlet rolled down the window. "You girls comin'? I want to get there before lunch. It's beef tips and gravy day. I don't know how much longer I'll be able to chew meat on my own, so I don't like to pass up the opportunity."

"My grandma used to say the same thing," Rosemarie said. "She was mad as heck when we had to start putting it in the blender."

"I've got plenty of room for your friend in the back,"

Scarlet said. "Unless you get carsick. This thing is brand new, and I'm a sympathetic vomiter."

"Oh, I'd love to come," Rosemarie called out. "I'd just need to stop by my place for some clothes. And I don't get carsick, but I do like to have travel snacks."

"Already got 'em," Scarlet said, shaking a plastic bag with what I assumed was her idea of essential car snacks for road trips to nudist colonies.

Rosemarie was halfway to the car, and I was still standing on the front porch with my mouth hanging open.

"This can't be happening," I said under my breath. "It can't, it can't, it can't."

I hurried after them, trying to figure out how things like this always ended up out of my control. I was the one with the expense account, the Lady Glock, and the P.I. license.

I'd barely tossed my bag in the back and climbed into the monster when Scarlet pressed her foot to the floor and took off. I grabbed the door handle with both hands and tried to pull it closed, the rain pelting me in the face. The only thing keeping me warm was the pure fear of falling out of the car and ending up like my mother's urn.

I managed to get the door shut and leaned back against the seat, sucking in deep breaths. I hurried and fastened my seatbelt as Scarlet ran a stop sign. The good news was that if we died before we got there I wouldn't have to get naked in front of a bunch of strangers.

"Here, put on a hat," Scarlet said, handing me a bright orange hat with an alligator on the front. "Your hair is so big I can't see out the passenger side window."

We stopped at Rosemarie's house and let her pack a bag. Neither of us had mentioned that she wouldn't need clothes where we were going, but I'd decided it was probably for the best. What Rosemarie didn't know wouldn't hurt her.

It took Rosemarie about seven minutes to change into a flirty white skirt with lace edges and an electric blue halter top that laced all the way down the front, showing an impressive amount of cleavage and just a peek of the thorny rose tattoo that wrapped around her left breast. She was wearing straw wedges and I could see her shivering outside from the warmth of the car. When Rosemarie took a vacation from school, she *really* took a vacation. I'd thought on more than one occasion that Rosemarie might have split personalities. Because one half of her closet looked as if it came out of the Sunday school teacher's catalogue. The other side looked like it came from the castoffs from Britney Spears's latest concert tour.

It took Rosemarie twenty-three more minutes to convince her neighbors to feed and walk her two Great Danes, Baby and Johnny Castle. Rosemarie and her dogs were close. Very close. I'd once seen her let Johnny Castle lick her in the mouth for twenty minutes. The problem was the dogs had a tendency to eat anyone who wasn't Rosemarie, so I could see the neighbor's reluctance to feed the dogs.

By the time Rosemarie made it back to the car, I'd eaten an entire can of cheddar cheese Pringles and Scarlet had fallen asleep. Her head slumped over the wheel and her eyelids hadn't closed all the way, so it looked like she was staring at me. The only reason I knew she was still alive was the soft snore that escaped every couple of minutes.

Rosemarie got back into the Hummer with a grunt, splashing little droplets of water everywhere.

"Lord, I'm tired of this rain," she said. "My hair hasn't looked good for two weeks. A little water and it goes flat as a pancake. Though I should probably be grateful it's not all huge like yours, Addison. Seagulls are going to try to land in your hair, thinking it's a nest."

"Thank you, Rosemarie," I said. "Have some chips." I tossed a bag of Cheetos into the back seat and heard the crackle of the bag as she ripped into it.

Scarlet let out an unladylike snort and her head popped up off the steering wheel. Her coifed hair stuck up on one side like she'd had electric shock therapy and her lipstick was smeared. Chip crumbs were scattered on the front of her shirt, and she looked a little disoriented and a lot crazy.

"Let's go," Scarlet said. "Time's a wastin'."

She threw the Hummer in reverse by accident and I

closed my eyes as we made contact with Rosemarie's garbage cans. Then she put it in drive and we hauled ass through Whiskey Bayou.

The drive to the Hidden Sunrise Naturist Community should've taken close to five hours. We made it in three and a half.

The sign wasn't flashy, but there was a guard stand and we had to show identification for him to open the gate. Scarlet was able to bring guests onto the resort as long as we abided by the rules. Which meant clothes weren't allowed, but participating in theme nights was encouraged.

The property itself was secluded by palm trees, and Scarlet managed to only hit the curb once as she took the winding road deep into the resort grounds.

"Wow," I said once the view cleared. "That's incredible."

It was ocean and beach for as far as the eye could see. If I wasn't so distracted by the naked people walking around the grounds, I could've really enjoyed myself.

"I think I'm confused," Rosemarie said, sticking her head between us in the front seat like a Golden Retriever. "Why are those people naked? Are we joining a cult? Because I did that once when I was nineteen and the hallucinogenics really messed with my head."

"This is a nudist colony," I said.

"Oh, all right then." She sat back in the seat like it was no big deal and I dug in my purse for one of the pills I'd snatched from my mom. I was going to need a little fortification before I started stripping down.

"Why is everyone carrying a towel?" I asked and then immediately regretted the question.

"It's a requirement here at the resort," Scarlet said. "You wouldn't want to sit in the same place some-one's naked parts have been. That would be gross."

"Right," I said. "What was I thinking?" And I was glad she'd explained. I wasn't too fond of the idea of putting my naked bits where someone else's naked bits might have been while I was eating beef tips and gravy for lunch.

We drove past a large two-story beach house that was built about ten feet off the ground. Stairs led up to the front of the house.

"The regular rooms and one of the restaurants are in there," Scarlet said. "They serve a buffet three times a day, and I guess it's okay if you like to get up and get your food for yourself."

"I don't," Rosemarie said. "If I'm going to go out to dinner I want to be served. It's the principle of the thing."

Scarlet and I nodded in agreement, and by the time we turned onto the winding beach road I was starting to feel the effects of the Xanax. I wasn't one to medicate often. I'd never done any kinds of drugs or had any kind of major surgery, but something as simple as a Midol made me a little loopy.

Scarlet parked the Hummer in front of a villa that was

bigger than my mother's house. It had a perfect view of the beach and was about twenty yards away from an identical villa on each side.

"That's Elmer's place down there," she said, pointing two villas down. "I scoped it out day before yesterday while he was playing dominoes. It's only a one-bedroom, so I'm wondering if he's as rich as he'd like me to believe. I don't even waste my time if their portfolio isn't double mine."

"Aunt Scarlet, he's a murderer," I said. "You can't possibly be considering him as husband material."

"A murderer?" Rosemarie squeaked. "That's what we're doing here?"

"Yes, a murderer," I said, thinking my voice was starting to sound a little bit like Charlie Brown's teacher. My tongue was numb.

"I'm not seriously considering him," Scarlet said. "But he's the one that got away. He bested me, the bastard. And I want revenge."

"You'd think capturing him and sending him off to prison would be enough," I said.

"Yeah, you'd think." Scarlet shrugged. "Addison, why do you keep smiling like that? It's a little creepy."

I could feel the smile, but I couldn't do anything about it. We all hopped out of the Hummer, and when I turned around to get my bag out of the back, I almost ran smack dab into a naked Rosemarie.

I might have passed out. I don't remember. But when I woke up I was lying on the ground and Scarlet was waving smelling salts under my nose.

"I'm fine," I said. "I think I just need to get some food in my stomach." I was lying. The last thing I wanted was food.

"We're just in time," Scarlet said. "I told you we'd make it for lunch if we hurried. You've got to take care of your body. I've lived on the same diet for ninety years and look at me. I'm fit as a fiddle. Hot cakes and bacon in the morning, along with two cups of Irish coffee. A nice protein lunch with a vegetable —preferably a potato—because that's the only vegetable worth eating in my opinion. And if you have vodka at lunch you get double the potatoes. A martini at three o'clock along with a Little Debbie Snack Cake. And then a nice home-cooked dinner that has some kind of gravy involved."

"What do you drink with dinner?" Rosemarie asked.

"I don't drink anything with dinner," Scarlet said. "But right after dinner I have three highballs because it helps me to get to sleep. I've got restless legs."

I was still lying on the ground and what I'd noticed from my new position was that Scarlet had disrobed as well. I wondered how long they'd left me on the ground while they'd gotten settled.

"Come on, girl," Scarlet said. "Get your clothes off and let's get to lunch. If we're lucky we might catch a glimpse of Elmer. The man likes his routine. He plays dominoes every morning after breakfast. And after lunch he likes to sun on one of the loungers down by the beach. I caught Rosemarie up on Elmer while you were out."

"Oh, good," I said, pushing myself to a standing position. My head was pounding and I wondered how hard I'd hit it.

"You probably got a good lump back there," Scarlet said. "You went down like a sack of potatoes."

I was starting to remember why. The sight of Rosemarie naked had taken me off guard. Not because it was Rosemarie naked. I was an adult and I could appreciate all shapes and sizes of the human body, even if I wasn't comfortable with displaying my own. It was the sheer whiteness of Rosemarie's flesh that had put me on my ass. She was the definition of the pure absence of color. I'd never seen anything as white as she was in my entire life. The combination of all that whiteness and the Xanax had made me think I was dying and going toward the white light. I'd just been taken by surprise.

"I can do this," I said, trying to convince myself that nothing was impossible when a hundred thousand dollars was on the line.

"Don't forget your flip-flops, sunscreen, and towel," Scarlet called after me as I went into the villa to change.

I found my suitcase in the guest bedroom and I quickly stripped down to nothing, not bothering to look at myself in the mirror. There was nothing I could do about my appearance. I couldn't fudge the extra cake I'd had at dinner two nights ago with Spanx, and I couldn't make my boobs seem like they were twenty-five again by wearing a push-up bra. The naked body told the honest truth.

Sometimes I wasn't a fan of the truth.

CHAPTER SIX

I WASN'T REALLY in the mood for beef tips and gravy, but Rosemarie and Aunt Scarlet seemed to have their hearts set on it, so I followed along, keeping my gaze averted as much as possible.

"Just a heads-up," Scarlet said. "Try not to stare at Marjorie when we go into the restaurant. She's got three boobs on account of she was in the circus."

"Right," I said. "No staring."

I decided the safest course of action was to order a salad and a mojito and pretend to be very interested in both. Keeping eye contact wasn't as simple as it seemed when I looked up and realized Rosemarie's breasts were sitting in her beef tips and gravy. It especially wasn't easy when she decided it was better to lick as much of the gravy off as possible instead of using her napkin. Which really told me two things about Rosemarie. 1.) She didn't like to let good gravy go to waste. And 2.) I'd never seen breasts as big as hers. It took a magical feat of engineering to be able to lift an entire breast to your mouth.

I might have snuck another one of my mother's magic pills. I've done a lot of things in my time as a private investigator. Things I'm not proud of and things that have made me uncomfortable. But this took the cake.

And then I realized what a failure I was at my job and I started to cry. Big, gasping sobs right there at the table.

"What the hell is wrong with you?" Scarlet asked. "Get a grip, girl. Holmeses don't cry. We get revenge and we do damage to people's cars. We don't shed tears. You're embarrassing me."

"I'm—I'm sorry," I gasped, crying even harder. "I don't know what's wrong."

"Christ, are you pregnant?" And then she called out to the waiter, "Can we get another mojito over here?"

"She's not pregnant," Rosemarie said. "But she's been popping little white pills since we left Georgia. I had to take some of those last year when Johnny Castle got hit by a car. I had no idea what had happened when my brain finally unfuzzed itself. All I know is I woke up in my recliner surrounded by about twelve pints of empty Häagen-Dazs cartons and I wasn't wearing anything but a Christmas garland and Tweety Bird slippers. That stuff makes you loopy."

I gave Rosemarie a lopsided smile and then started

crying again. "My life is a mess. Why can't I make a simple decision? I want to get married. I don't want to grow old alone. But I'm terrified. I get heart palpitations just thinking about it."

"That's good," Scarlet said. "Because marriage *is* terrifying. My third husband tried to poison me and steal all my money. But karma showed him. He ended up falling off his horse and breaking his neck. So it all works out in the end."

My sobs had turned into sniffles while I tried to process Scarlet's words of wisdom. It was mostly giving me a headache so I focused instead on the fresh mojito.

"I'm fine," I said. "I just want to catch Elmer and get out of here. I've got the picture of his tattoo that Savage sent me, and I'm ready to do this thing. I'm not meant to be naked all the time, I like accessories too much. And it's really disconcerting to see that man eating ribs over there while his junk is free-styling under the table. Maybe we can hit the outlet on the way home and I can buy some new shoes."

"There you go," Scarlet said. "There's that Holmes spirit. Focus on the outcome and the reward. You've got a fat wad of cash waiting for you at the end of this and a pair of Louboutins with your name on them."

"I can only afford Louboutins if I buy them out of the trunk of someone's car," I said.

"Not this time. This time you're buying the real

thing. The reward has to be equal to the risk. And this time the risk is Louboutin levels."

I thought about that for a second and it seemed like sound logic to me. "Let's go catch a murderer."

———

THE ONLY THING I had to go by was Elmer Hughes's driver's license picture. And I hated to admit it, but there was something about really old people that made it hard to distinguish between them—men and women alike, they all looked the same. And unfortunately, they didn't photograph genitalia at the DMV, because that might've made it a little easier.

"Lord, would you look at the testicles on that man," Aunt Scarlet said. "They're the size of oranges. How do you think he keeps from sitting on them?"

"You think he's had implants?" Rosemarie asked. "I've heard plastic surgeons down here make a killing on senior citizens. People get to a certain age and then want to discover the fountain of youth."

"And testicular implants are supposed to make you look younger?" I asked skeptically, trying to zoom in on Elmer.

"Everything droops when you get to be my age," Scarlet said. "We always associate tight and firm with youthfulness. Instead of getting the implants, he should've given those puppies a facelift. They almost hang all the way to his knees. I thought he was going to trip over them the other day out on the golf course."

Elmer was down on the beach under one of the umbrellas, sunning on a lounger top side up, making sure his oranges got plenty of exposure. I could barely get a decent shot of the tattoo on his arm, and even with the full zoom and focus of the camera, it was still difficult to make out. Age hadn't been kind to Elmer.

"I thought about getting my lady parts tightened up a bit," Scarlet continued. "They call it vaginal rejuvenation, if you can believe that. I haven't had anything rejuvenating down there since the time I walked through Wally Pinkerton's yard and all the sprinklers came on."

"Umm," I said, for lack of anything better.

"I was going to get rejuvenated because a couple of years ago I thought I might be getting some action, and I wanted everything to look as if it just came out of the factory. But the fellow up and died on me before we could get all hot and bothered. Take my advice, Addison. Never let a man die when they're lying on top of you. Thank God he was wearing one of those medic alert buttons around his neck, because I never would've been able to push him off to reach the phone."

I was in a complete state of Zen. The mojito and the Xanax were magical and I could feel nothing in my brain or my body.

"It's probably best you opted out of the surgery,"

Rosemarie said. "Sharon Osbourne said it was excruciating."

"Ehh, I don't have much feeling left down there anyway," Scarlet said with a shrug. "I've stopped holding out hope."

"You've just got to wait for a man who's big enough to make things seem not so loosey-goosey down there."

"I'm going to have to get closer," I said, hoping this would distract them from the conversation.

"Look," Rosemarie said. "Those loungers right next to him just came open. Let's get them before someone else does. You should be able to take plenty of pictures from that angle."

"I still don't understand how you could recognize the tattoo," I said to Scarlet. "It's so wrinkled and distorted it's nearly impossible to make out."

"Some things you don't forget," she said sagely. "The Whiskey Bayou bank robbery of '43 and a Latin lover named Mario are the two things that stick with me the most. Whew, was your Uncle Stan steamed about Mario. But once I explained he was Spanish royalty and it was an honor to be asked to sleep with him, Stan calmed right down." She looked confused for a minute and slapped her hand on top of her head to keep her hat from blowing away. "May he rest in peace."

Rosemarie and I stared at Scarlet with horrified fascination, and I did a half-assed sign of the cross along with Rosemarie and Scarlet at the mention of Uncle Stanley's untimely demise. Stanley had been her fifth and final husband, but he'd died when I was a kid so I barely remembered him.

We made our way to the stairs that led down to the beach, and I immediately noticed the little tiki hut bar set up about twenty feet behind Elmer. *A private investigator, a choir teacher, and a geriatric spy walk into a bar...* No one would have ever believed it.

We spread our towels out on the loungers, adjusted the umbrellas so we were protected from direct sunlight, and got comfortable. I set the camera on the little table next to the loungers and pointed it at Elmer, who seemed to be snoozing peacefully on the lounger a few feet away.

The problem with the camera was that it made noise when pictures were taken, and I didn't know how sound of a sleeper Elmer was. So I used my second best option and pulled out my iPhone.

The beach waiter came up and took our drink orders, and I sighed, frustrated, because I couldn't get a clear shot of the tattoo on Elmer's arm with my phone. I had to have the tattoo. It was the only documented proof the FBI had of the Romeo Bandit. And if I wanted a big reward, I had to have definite proof.

I watched Elmer for ten more minutes and contemplated my choices while I sipped on a Sex on the Beach. Rosemarie was reading a book two loungers over, and Aunt Scarlet had gotten bored and was building a sand castle, wearing nothing but a big hat and a lot of sand she was probably going to regret getting up close and personal with later.

"Don't forget the sunscreen, Aunt Scarlet," I called out a little too loud, watching Elmer closely to see if he stirred. Nope. He was down for the count. It was now or never.

I took another fortifying sip of my drink and grabbed the camera. I put the strap around my neck and got on all fours in the hot sand. I might have muttered an expletive or two, having not thought through the fact that it would feel like dipping my hands and knees in molten glass.

I tried not to think about what I looked like from behind. And then I did think about it and grabbed the towel off my lounger, draping it across my backside like a tablecloth. I snuck a quick look at the bartender at the tiki hut bar, but while I'd been contemplating my course of action, Rosemarie had decided her own course of action. She had the naked bartender cornered, a guy of about twenty-five or so, and he looked both horrified and fascinated at the same time. Rosemarie had her own brand of magic when it came to men. She'd once caused a man to be in traction for six weeks during a tantric sex marathon.

The bartender was easy pickins. And he was most definitely distracted. I slowly crawled on hands and knees until I was inches away from Elmer Hughes.

My heart was pounding in my chest and I was covered with sweat and sand, neither of my favorite things. I realized my buzz and the Xanax must have worn off, because I was feeling a whole lot of anxiety all of a sudden.

Elmer let out a soft snore and I squeaked. His arm was limp and his hands were gnarled with age. He wore a pinky ring with a small ruby in the center. The tattoo was wrinkled and the ink had faded over the years, but now that I was up close, I could see it clearly. A thorny vine and rosary beads were twined around a naked woman that had more curves than Kim Kardashian. The vine and the rosary beads ended at the top of his hand where the rose had started to bloom. And right between the woman's legs was the name *Romeo*.

I'd found him. The Romeo Bandit was alive and well after all these years. And he was about to get taken down by three naked women. That was going to sting. Elmer struck me as the type of guy who'd want to be taken down by a man.

I brought the camera up and took a couple of quick shots, and then I bit my lip as I debated whether or not to stretch his skin out a little and get a more complete picture. I finally decided that was the alcohol talking and probably not the best decision, and then I realized the alcohol had been giving me direction through this whole debacle because what I was doing definitely wasn't using my best judgment.

I found this out the hard way when I turned to crawl back to my own lounger and my towel got stuck under my knee, pulling it completely off and leaving me bare-assed with my lady bits flapping in the breeze.

"Yikes," a male voice said behind me.

I scrambled to cover my rear with the towel and turned my head in time to catch Elmer Hughes's horrified stare.

"Jesus God," he wheezed, clutching his chest. "I thought I was having a flashback from the seventies. Those things looked a lot different then. That's nothing like '70s bush. You've got a nice landscaper."

I turned fifty shades of red and scrambled to make sure I was completely covered with the towel. And then I noticed his gaze had shifted to the camera in my hand.

"I can explain," I said. "I was putting on sunscreen and it made my ring loose, and it flew right off my hand and under your lounge chair. My camera has a light and a magnifier on it, so I thought maybe I'd be able to see it better."

Holy shit. I could lie like a boss. I had no idea where that came from, but even *I* believed it, I was so convincing. Maybe it was the Xanax/mojito cocktail that made me such a great liar.

"Huh," Elmer said. "Did you find it?"

"No. And boy is my husband going to be pissed. That's the second time I've lost a wedding ring."

"Maybe it's a sign from God you're not supposed to be married," he said, waggling big bushy eyebrows.

My lips curled in disgust and I chose that unfortunate

moment to look at Elmer's oranges. It turned out there was still some life down there after all.

"Impressive, isn't it?" he said.

"Yep, just what I was thinking." I crawled forward another inch, thinking of escape and someone to call for help. Lying had gotten me in a lot of trouble. And I wasn't willing to do anything for a hundred thousand dollars after all.

I searched for Rosemarie and was just in time to see her and the bartender disappear behind the bar in a tangle of limbs. I searched for Aunt Scarlet, but she'd buried herself in the sand and was busy building anatomically incorrect breasts on her chest. I had no backup and there was no rescue in sight.

"How about you join me for dinner tonight? I can arrange a private meal in my villa at sunset, overlooking the ocean. Do you like roses?"

I could see how he'd seduced hundreds of women. There was a certain debonair charm about him that was appealing, even though he was long past his prime. He must've been lethal back in the day. No woman would've been able to resist.

"I love roses," I managed to say. "And I'd love to have dinner."

"Good. I'm in number one twenty-seven. Just come around to the back deck."

He lay back down and closed his eyes and I let out a sign of relief. I crawled the rest of the way to my lounger and started gathering up my stuff. I was pretty much exhausted for the day, and I needed a nap in hopes that a good idea about how to capture him would appear somewhere in my dreams. Because at the moment, I had nothing. I'd left my cuffs in Whiskey Bayou by accident, and I was pretty sure using the Glock in my beach bag would get me arrested since I was in another state and I didn't have any authority here. Not that I had a lot of authority back home, but at least most of the cops knew me and cut me some slack.

I was going to need help. Of the professional kind. Savage was never going to let me live this down.

CHAPTER SEVEN

CALLING Savage was the last thing I wanted to do. And when I say the last thing, I mean that I'd rather be tied to the stake with fire licking at the bottom of my feet than have to face him. But I needed help, and we had a very short window of time to make the capture.

Savage was like a temptation test from God. At least that's the way I'd decided to look at it. I wasn't sure if I'd passed any of His other tests, but I was batting a thousand on this one. I'd managed to say no every time Savage had made a move, and I still didn't understand where I'd gathered the inner resolve.

I loved Nick. I mean really loved him. There probably weren't a lot of men out there that were willing to put up with P.I. girlfriends who were only average at their job. Not to mention the fact that trouble seemed to follow me wherever I went. I often wondered why a guy like Nick could love me. He was beautiful to look at—the body of a swimmer and a face sculpted by Michelangelo. He was a damned good cop, and I hadn't even found out that he was filthy rich until we'd been dating for months. It hadn't mattered. Nick had a code, and that's what I loved about him. And he always had my back.

Savage made Nick look like second-string quarterback. The man oozed testosterone, and I'd once had to check my underwear to see if he'd made it disintegrate. He was part Native American and part Greek god, and I was willing to bet Savage had no problems with anyone seeing him naked.

But we were all adults and a lot was at stake, so I sent him a picture I'd taken of the tattoo and made the call to ask for the biggest favor of my life. Not much phased Savage, so he said he'd be on the next flight and would see me before my dinner date. I was pretty sure this might be the last time we ever worked together, because I wouldn't be able to face him again after he saw me naked.

I'd spent the afternoon napping, and when I woke up I was sunburned and I had a hangover. I stumbled into the bathroom and stuck my head in the faucet, drinking water right out of the tap. And then I looked up and saw myself in the mirror and screamed.

No one came running in to see what was wrong, so I figured they'd already seen me and didn't want to be frightened again, or no one was in the villa. I took a shower and then toweled off gently, admiring the pale strips of skin that ran down the middle of my boobs from where the camera strap had hung. The skin on either side was bright pink.

I rubbed lotion all over my body and was grateful it would be dark by the time I had to go to dinner because there wasn't a lot I could do to spruce myself up other than hide in the shadows. I did spend the half hour it took to blow dry and straighten my hair, and I dabbed concealer under my eyes and a few other places to get rid of the green tinge left by the hangover.

By the time I walked into the main living area I was feeling mostly human.

"I thought I heard you scream," Scarlet said, pinning a big Hawaiian flower in her hair. She wore a grass hula skirt and a lei dangled between her ninety-year-old breasts.

"Figured you must've woken up and saw yourself in the mirror. You gave me a pretty good fright too when I came in and saw you on the bed. Thought you were dead. Or maybe one of those zombies that I'd have to shoot in the head with a shotgun."

"I'm glad you refrained," I said dryly. "I've got a date with Elmer tonight."

Rosemarie was freshening her lipstick, and I recognized the relaxed, satisfied glow of a woman who'd spent the afternoon being horizontal with a man. Her hair was back to perfect Farrah Fawcett curls and she was dressed just like Scarlet, only her grass skirt didn't cover as much real estate.

"We know," Rosemarie said. "You kept muttering about it in your sleep. Something about being seduced by working oranges."

"Why are y'all leaving? We've got to capture Elmer tonight. I can't do it by myself."

"We can't all go to Elmer's for dinner," Scarlet said. "He's an old man. You'll be able to take him down easy. Remember to go for the little bones. Hurts like a bitch. Besides, it's a luau theme tonight down at the beach. We don't want to miss that. They're giving away those little pineapple drinks with the umbrellas."

"I can't believe y'all aren't going to have my back," I said. "We're supposed to be a team. What if he pulls a gun? Or tries some funny business?"

Rosemarie looked at Scarlet. "I told you she was going to make us go with her."

Scarlet sighed and put her hands on her hips. "What'll you give us if we go with you?"

The hangover was making my stomach pitch and my head was pounding. I was feeling aggravated and a little bit mean. I narrowed my eyes. "How about I let you collect your share of the million-dollar reward instead of bashing you over the head and taking it from you?"

"Million-dollar reward," Rosemarie said. "Nobody told me that. What's my cut?"

"Your cut comes out of Scarlet's take," I said before Scarlet could answer.

"I told you you were a Holmes through and through," Scarlet said. "I can't believe you'd take an old lady's money."

"I don't think you're an old lady. I think you're the Devil in an old lady suit."

Scarlet cackled and her hula skirt rustled. "Don't you know it, girlie. I'm too bad to die. Nobody wants me. Not even the Devil himself."

"Good, I'm glad that's settled," I said. "Let's get moving. You can go to the luau after we're done. I just want someone watching from outside in case things get out of hand."

I checked my phone, but I didn't have any messages from Savage. I'd given him the address and Elmer's villa number, but we were getting down to crunch time and I was wondering if I was going to be flying solo when it came to making the collar. I couldn't see Rosemarie and Scarlet being a lot of help.

"Small bones," I said under my breath.

"There you go," Scarlet said, and we headed out the door to go catch a murderer.

———

THE SUN HAD STARTED its descent and the paths between the buildings were already dark, so tiki torches had been placed to light the way. I walked to Elmer's in my flip-flops and the lei Rosemarie had put over my head as we walked out the door. Oddly enough, the lei made it feel like I almost had clothes on, so I was walking with a little more confidence, not caring that Rosemarie and Scarlet were following my shining pink behind from somewhere in the distance.

They weren't too far back because I could hear them muttering and clomping through the palm fronds. I wasn't sure what kind of spy Scarlet had been during the war, but it must not have been the silent type.

"There you are," Elmer said from somewhere to my left.

I almost jumped out of my skin. He was standing in the shadows and I hadn't heard him at all. I needed to focus. I was *not* going to be outsmarted by a ninety-something lothario. That would be embarrassing.

"Oh, you scared me. I was in my own world."

"It's easy to do that here," he said, holding out his hand and helping me up the stairs to his back deck. Lanterns were placed so the deck was awash in a romantic light and the sun reflected off the waves. It would have been an awesome sight any other time or with just about any other person.

I'd managed to keep my gaze at eye level. I wasn't interested in seeing a repeat performance of what had happened down at the beach, and the squishy feeling in my stomach had intensified by about a million. I'd left my Glock back at Scarlet's, but I knew Scarlet was armed and Rosemarie was carrying zip ties in case I needed restraints.

They must've found a good hiding place, because I hadn't heard a peep from them since Elmer came out of the shadows. My breath hitched when Elmer brought his other hand from behind his back, but I released it with a nervous laugh when I saw the long-stemmed red rose he held.

"A beautiful flower for a beautiful lady," he said, bowing slightly.

Thank God it was almost dark, because I'd hate to call a man a liar. Don't get me wrong, I was more than passable in the looks department. I even had days when the hair and makeup and water retention gods were all working in my favor and I felt beautiful. Today wasn't one of those days. I was sunburned and hungover and I had a pooch from all the alcohol I'd drunk. Those fruity drinks had a lot of calories.

"Thank you," I said with all the cheerfulness I could muster. And then I made the mistake of looking past him and into his villa. I could see straight into his bedroom. Candles were lit all over the room—to the point I was afraid the entire place was going to go up in flames—and the bed was turned back and rose petals scattered across the sheets.

My lungs constricted and little black dots danced in front of my eyes. "What's for dinner?" I managed to say.

"I thought we might have some champagne and get to know each other a little better first."

His finger touched the back of my hand and I felt the

gorge rise up in my throat. I was about at the end of my rope.

"Small bones," I muttered.

"What's that?" he asked.

"Never mind. Listen, Elmer—"

"I don't recall telling you my name," he said, dark eyes narrowing into a menacing stare.

"I'm here with my Aunt Scarlet. She mentioned your name when I told her where I was going for dinner."

Damn, I still had the good lie juju. I was starting to become impressed with myself.

"Yes, yes," he said. "Scarlet. I once knew a woman named Scarlet a long, long time ago. She seduced me and then broke my heart." He smiled, his capped teeth eerily white and even in the fading sunlight. "I remember her fondly."

"Hmm, yes. Well—" I struggled for the words and just decided to go for it. The tattoo matched and there was no time like the present. I just had to figure out where to touch him. I didn't want to grab the wrong limb by mistake in the takedown.

"Are your bones fairly strong?" I asked.

"Beg your pardon?"

"Your bones," I repeated. "You think they're pretty strong?"

"This is a very unusual conversation. A little exciting." He waggled his eyebrows creepily. "Are you going to hurt me?"

"Eww," I said. "Not that way." I took Elmer by the wrist and squeezed, using a technique Savage had taught me back when we were in and out of each other's pockets. Elmer screamed like a little girl and went to his knees, and I twisted his arm behind his back.

"Hush," I hissed, putting my other hand over his mouth so no one would hear his scream.

I put my knee in his back like I'd seen the cops do and then I realized I was practically straddling Elmer while buck-ass naked.

"I need restraints," I called out. But Rosemarie and Scarlet didn't come out of the bushes.

"What are you doing?" Elmer said. "I'm not into the kinky stuff. I'm too old. I've got a pacemaker."

"I told you to hush," I said. "Elmer Hughes, you should've kept the tattoo hidden a little longer. Like until you died. Or should I call you the Romeo Bandit?"

He went still beneath me and I grabbed his other arm to pull behind his back. "Rosemarie," I called out a little louder this time. "I'm not playing. I need the restraints."

"I don't know what you're talking about," Elmer said. "But I demand that you unhand me. I'm a paying member of this resort and they have rules here. You're sexually assaulting me, you reprobate. It's wrong to take advantage of a senior citizen just because his plumbing still works."

"Don't flatter yourself," I said. "*Rosemarie!*" I yelled louder. "If you don't get out here right now I'm never watching *Real Housewives* with you again."

"I sent Rosemarie and Scarlet down to the luau," Savage said, stepping out from the shadows, a big smile on his face.

"Oh, Jesus God," I said, letting go of Elmer and slapping my hand over my eyes. I felt Elmer roll away from me and get up, but then I heard a couple of grunts and peeked through my fingers to see Elmer back on the ground with cuffs around his wrists.

"What are you doing?" Savage asked.

"Sorry," I said. "I panicked. I thought you were naked and I couldn't handle it."

He laughed out loud and I felt ridiculous all of a sudden. And then I remembered I was the one that was naked. Savage had on jeans and a t-shirt and his gun.

"I'm not sure *I* can handle it," he said, his voice deepening. "I've got to tell you I've had a lot of fantasies that involved this moment."

"You had fantasies about us at a nudist colony?"

"No, just about us being naked. Together."

I had a hot flash and started waving my hand in front of my face. "You can't do this. We had a truce."

"That was before I saw you naked. And Addison, the fantasies don't measure up to the reality."

"Nope, nope, nope. I'm not listening." I stuck my fingers in my ears like a toddler and tried not to pay attention to the fact that my nipples had hardened like tiny pebbles.

"You're very good at this," Elmer told Savage. "Nice technique."

"Thank you," Savage said. "Elmer Hughes, you're under arrest for the murder of twenty-two people, plus committing multiple armed robberies as the Romeo Bandit."

"I'd rather you just shoot me if you don't mind. I'm not a fan of prison."

"I wouldn't mind putting a bullet in you," Scarlet said, coming out of the shadows and up on the deck to stand over Elmer.

"Jesus," Savage said, looking at Scarlet in her full glory. His gaze seemed to be fixed on the hot-pink pubic hair, and I couldn't say I blamed him. It was mesmerizing.

"Scarlet?" Elmer asked. "What the hell do you want to put a bullet in me for? We're neighbors. I thought you were just a desperate old lady."

"I've never been desperate. Not even when you seduced me the first time. I almost cut you loose back then when you started talking about your wife. Really killed the mood. But you made up for it later. I have to say you were one of the best."

"Of course I was. Still am. You can't possibly be *that* Scarlet. She was one of the most beautiful creatures I've ever seduced. There was no one comparable to her in bed."

"Yes, I know. And I've hardly changed at all, so I don't appreciate your insults."

Savage and I shared a look that said it all. Scarlet was delusional. And this was ridiculous. Three-fourths of us were naked and I was kind of tired of being at the naked party.

"After all these years you're getting just what you deserve," Scarlet said. "You might be a charming Romeo, but you're still a killer. And you still have to pay." She turned to Savage and said, "Maybe you could rough him up a little on the way in. Say he resisted or something."

"He's an old man," Savage said. "He has to pee every ten minutes. That's punishment enough."

"I want to go home now. And I want to wear clothes," I said. "I also want my reward money so I can buy some new shoes. This has been a trying twenty-four hours."

"You're welcome to come back with me," Savage said. "We can drop Elmer in for booking and then hit the outlet mall on the way back to Savannah."

"You're a good friend," I said.

Savage raised a brow and the smile he gave me sent a shiver all the way to my lady bits. "The clothing part is optional," he said.

Decisions, decisions.

The End

WHISKEY TANGO FOXTROT

Available Now - Whiskey Tango Foxtrot

THERE ARE some days it's not worth getting out of bed. Today was one of those days.

Sirens blared in the distance, but between tourist traffic and people generally being assholes and not moving to the side of the road for emergency responders, I figured the cops still had a good five minutes before they got here.

A hysterical woman was Skyping with someone from Channel 8 News, reporting that shots had been fired at the Enmark Gas Station off Montgomery Street. Rosemarie and I had pulled up just in time to see the woman put on fresh lipstick and practice a couple of sobs before dialing into the station.

Over the last several years, Savannah's crime had spiked. Shootings and domestic disturbance calls were always going out over the radio. And this was the third gas station robbery this week. The cops were doing everything they could to keep things under control, but like with most things, when politicians got involved everything went down the shitter. So while the cops worked with their hands halfway tied behind their backs and buried in mountains of red tape, dodging bullets and putting their lives in danger, the rest of us got to watch the city burn. So to speak.

Shots rang out from inside the gas station and everyone hit the deck, myself included.

"Shoot that motherfucker!" Rosemarie screamed, a hysterical tinge to her voice.

We huddled behind the open doors of her bright yellow Beetle. On her best day, Rosemarie didn't do well in stressful situations. She'd shown up at the detective agency about half an hour ago, her mascara smudged from the night before and her bright red dress turned inside out. Her hair looked like she'd brushed it with a hand mixer, and I was almost a hundred percent sure she wasn't wearing a bra. Using the deductive reasoning skills I'd acquired over the two months I'd been a private investigator, I was willing to go out on a limb and say today was nowhere near one of her "best days."

"Ssh," I hissed. "You don't want to startle him into killing anyone."

"He's killing everyone. Didn't you just hear him unloading on all those poor people? They're just trying to get their gas station Danishes and fill up their tanks for a nice weekend away. And now they're all going to die." Rosemarie inhaled a deep breath and let out a *hee-hee-hoo* like she was in Lamaze class. Rosemarie was a little excitable.

"He's not killing everyone. He just fired a bunch of rounds into the ceiling. Kid can't be more than twenty. Looks scared to death."

"America's youth today," she said, shaking her head. "Be glad you're not teaching anymore. Everything's going to hell in a handbasket. I had a kid tell me the other day that Disney invented Pocahontas because they needed a Native American princess, and that she wasn't a real person like Wikipedia claimed. Took everything I had not to slap him right upside the head. In two years he's probably going to be holding up a gas station too. And what is that boy wearing? He's robbing a gas station convenience store in his pajama pants? And plaid pajamas at that. I hate to break it to him, but he looks like the *Brawny* lumber- jack instead of a badass."

"Maybe he thought the wife beater and bandana tied around his head made him look tough enough."

"You'd think they'd have some kind of online classes for thugs," she said. "They've got online classes for just about everything these days. Some enterprising young man could monetize the site and probably make a fortune off all the gangbangers and lowlifes, teaching them how to commit crime more efficiently."

"I'm sure the Better Business Bureau would love that," I said dryly.

"Are you going to shoot him or not? I'm starting to get a cramp and I need a fucking donut."

"You sure are swearing a lot today. That's not like you."

"I've been watching marathons of *Mad Men*. It's a bad influence on my social niceties."

"I can't shoot anyone," I said. "I left my gun in the shower caddy at the office."

For the last week, I'd been calling the McClean Detective Agency my home. I'd been living with Nick Dempsey for several months before he decided to ask me to marry him and threw a wrench in the works. I'll admit I panicked. A girl who's been left at the altar doesn't think about marriage and weddings without fear rearing its ugly head. I thought I'd been very mature when I told him I needed time to think on it, and that maybe it was best if we gave each other a little space while I did.

In reality, I'd been avoiding Nick like the plague. Our lines of work often put us in each other's paths, but I had Nick radar. I could practically feel his presence before he ever arrived at a scene. I could also feel his presence because I'd stuck one of the trackers we used at the agency underneath his truck. My phone vibrated every time he was in a ten-mile radius.

It was really hard to give myself the space I needed to make an informed, adult decision. I knew what that man could do in bed, and my hormones weren't as informed and adult as my brain was.

"We're all going to die," Rosemarie said. "Help me, Jesus. Help me!" She threw in a sign of the cross for good measure. Rosemarie was Methodist just like I was, but I figured God might give her extra points for effort.

"Oh, for Pete's sake," I mumbled under my breath. Then I reached into the car and grabbed the box of donuts we'd just procured when the call for the robbery had come through on the police scanner. I slid the box toward Rosemarie and she huddled behind the door, her blue eyes wide and round like a Kewpie doll, as she devoured a chocolate glazed.

I still wasn't sure why Rosemarie had a police scanner in her car. Or where she'd gotten it, for that matter. Rosemarie taught choir at James Madison High School in Whiskey Bayou, but ever since I'd gotten my P.I. license she liked to think of us as the Southern version of Cagney and Lacey, even though she had no special training and had a tendency to overreact in high stress situations. In reality, we were more like a deranged Abbott and Costello.

"I'm just saying," Rosemarie said, reaching for another donut, "what good is a gun if you're going to leave it in the shower? I've got mine right under the front seat of the car. You can use it if you want to."

"I'll pass," I said. "The police will be here soon." Not to mention the fact that I was pretty sure Rosemarie didn't have a concealed carry permit. But that didn't stop ninety percent of the Georgia population from carrying them anyway. Southerners weren't fond of things like permits.

"Why do you take your gun in the shower anyway?" she asked.

"I take my gun everywhere," I said, peeping around the car door to look inside the gas station so I could assess the situation. The more information I could give the cops when they arrived the better. "But I wasn't expecting you to use the spare key and disarm the agency alarms while I was trying to put my clothes on. And I sure wasn't expecting you to burst into the bathroom and drag me half-naked down the hall because you were having a crisis. So it got left in the shower caddy."

"I needed a donut," she said, pouting a little. "I had a rough night. I thought Robbie might be the one. After Leroy broke my heart I did what I read in Cosmo and had a couple of rebound flings. Then I met Robbie and my world tilted on its axis and all thoughts of Leroy went right out the window. I thought that was a sign that I'd found *the one*. And it was my first attempt at being a cougar."

"Who's Robbie?" I asked.

"He's that bartender we met last week at the nudist colony."

"Don't remind me," I groaned.

A week ago, I'd caught my first and last case that involved going undercover at a nudist colony. The experience had taught me a lot about myself. Mostly that I wasn't meant to be naked at the beach. There were parts of the body that shouldn't be exposed to sand and sun. I'd also discovered that I didn't particularly want to see other people naked either. There was nothing quite like watching the woman across the dinner table as her nipple fell into her soup bowl every time she leaned forward.

"You thought Robbie was the one?" I asked, perplexed. "You hadn't talked to him five minutes before y'all were going at it behind the tiki bar. How are you supposed to know someone's *the one* after five minutes? And three and a half of that was foreplay."

Rosemarie sniffed. "Sometimes souls just connect. It was like that for me and Robbie. But being at a nudist colony really takes away the subtleties of flirtation. I could see everything he was thinking below his waist. It's hard not to fall for such blatant seduction techniques."

"I take it Robbie doesn't share your soulmate sensibilities?"

"Robbie graduated from high school last year and still lives with his parents. They all live full-time at the nudist colony. He's not sure about working and living out in the real world. He said he likes the freedom of the nudist lifestyle and he'll miss his mother's chocolate chip cookies if he moves away from her."

"Jesus," I said, eyes wide. "He's practically an infant. Men don't know anything about pleasing women at that age."

Rosemarie frowned and said, "I've slept with a lot of men. I'm not sure I've ever found one that knew how to please me. I think it's a myth. Like unicorns. Or that picture that went viral on Facebook about the man with two penises. Anyone could see that second one was Photoshopped."

"Men that know how to please women exist," I said glumly.

I knew this because I'd just told one I had to think about an eternity of receiving pleasure. I was an idiot. I looked at Rosemarie and felt indignation rise up within me that none of her partners had been interested in anything but their own pleasure.

"You're a woman in the prime of your life," I told her. "What you need is a *real* man. An older man. Someone who knows how to treat you outside the bedroom and rock your world inside it. Maybe a widower or a divorcee."

"Where do you think I can find one of those?" she asked, intrigued. "Assisted living? Or maybe that retirement village down on Tybee Island? They're real go getters down there."

I didn't really have a solution. Indignation was about as far as I could take this particular problem. "Have you tried one of the online dating sites?"

"Oh, sure. I've got profiles on all of them. Everyone lies about who they are and what they look like, and when you finally meet in person you know you're only meeting for a quick hookup, so no one much cares about the lies anyway."

"That's horrible," I said, my faith in humanity

slightly dented. "They always show those people getting married and so happy on the commercials."

"I think mostly they're happy they're getting regular sex and didn't marry a serial killer. Those computer programs are pretty good at screening out most of the crazies. At least the ones that might kill you."

"Huh," I said and turned my attention back to the gas station. No more shots had been fired and the sirens were getting closer. I took a deep breath and peeked around the side of the door so I could look into the gas station one more time.

I wasn't sure what I'd been mentally preparing myself to see. I was past thirty, so it was understandable that my eyes might not have been as good as they once were. In fact, I was praying that was the case. There had to be a thousand or so ninety-something women who wore fur coats over their velour jogging suits. There was no reason to think that my Aunt Scarlet was inside the gas station with an armed robber. She was supposed to be halfway to Italy on a singles cruise.

I peeped again and sighed. My eyesight was spectacular. And there was no mistaking Aunt Scarlet.

"Hey," Rosemarie said, coming back to rational behavior as the sugar hit her bloodstream. "That looks just like Scarlet. I thought she was headed out on a single's cruise."

"That was the plan," I said. "Maybe it's not her."

It was her. There was no mistaking Aunt Scarlet. In

her prime, people said that Scarlet looked just like Ava Gardner. I'd seen pictures, so I knew the rumors to be true. I'm not sure what had happened as the years passed, but Ava Gardner started looking more like Mickey Rooney. She'd shrunk, so she was barely five-feet tall, and she had a shock of white hair she kept permed and teased so it added a couple inches to her height. She kept it shellacked so nothing less than hurricane-force winds could move it out of place. She was wearing a mink, floor-length coat that swallowed her and she looked mad as hell.

Scarlet Holmes was my father's aunt. She'd grown up in Whiskey Bayou and outlived five husbands, a couple we weren't so sure had died of natural causes. Most families had a skeleton or two in the closet. Scarlet was one of ours. She liked her men young, her whiskey neat, and her cigarette's unfiltered.

"Thank you. I feel better now," Rosemarie said, pushing the half empty box of donuts back toward me. "It's the stress. It makes me irrational. I've got a new game plan now. I won't even look at a man unless he's on the sunny side of sixty. Maybe Scarlet knows someone."

"Maybe you should get some anti-anxiety meds," I told her.

"I've got some, but I don't like being that relaxed. Two days before Christmas I was stressed because the home spa I'd ordered for my mother showed delayed shipping. And you know how my mother is. I'd never have heard the end of it to show up to Christmas dinner without *everyone's* gifts. So I schlepped myself to the mall two freaking days before Christmas. Holiday shopping always makes me a little crazy anyway, so I popped a couple of those pills and ended up taking a nap on one of the display couches in JCPenney. Turns out they thought I was dead and called 9-1-1."

I was only half-listening to Rosemarie. Pretty much nothing she said shocked me anymore. I was more interested in how to get my Aunt Scarlet out of the gas station alive. She was standing face to face with the gunman, but neither of them were speaking. The situation looked tense.

If I hadn't been so focused on Scarlet and the gunman I would've felt my phone vibrate, signaling Nick's arrival. The second his hand touched my shoulder chills danced along my spine and my nipples went to full alert.

"Any donuts left?" he asked.

I'd forgotten how to blink, and I was starting to get a cramp in my calf from squatting too long. His voice rasped across my skin and my hand clutched the seat. I mentally ran down what I looked like. And winced.

I hadn't been kidding when I'd said Rosemarie had dragged me down the hall half-naked. I'd had time to put on a pair of black sweatpants, a thermal under-shirt and an oversized Georgia Tech sweatshirt I'd had since college. I hadn't actually gone to Georgia Tech, but I'd dated a guy who had. It turns out I liked the sweatshirt much more than the guy, so I'd kept it.

What I wasn't wearing, however, was a bra or underwear. Rosemarie hadn't had time to wait for those niceties. She'd needed donuts. I'd barely had time to slip my feet into black UGGs (without socks) and the down-quilted, black coat I'd gotten on sale at Eddie Bauer. My hair had been damp, so I'd braided it and pulled a hot pink, wool watch cap down over my ears. My face was scrubbed clean, and if I'd been buying booze instead of donuts I would've gotten carded for sure.

In other words, I didn't look my best. And Nick always looked amazing. He was movie star handsome, with dark hair, swarthy skin, and the kind of bones that only came from someone of good breeding. His eyes were the color of arctic waters, and every time he took his clothes off I wanted to jump his bones. Fortunately, he liked having his bones jumped. Otherwise, I'd probably be in jail for sexual harassment.

His entire family was filthy rich and his grandfather was a senator. And other than his grandfather, I'd never met people more awful than Nick's family. Someday they'd be giving Satan tips on how to run hell.

I kept my gaze straight ahead. "Help yourself," I said, blindly handing him the almost-empty box.

I stared at the inside of the car door, and focused on keeping my breathing steady. I was afraid if I turned around and looked at him it would be like staring at the sun and I might go blind.

I hadn't been expecting Nick to arrive at the scene.

He was homicide. And it seemed like someone was always getting murdered in Savannah, so it was a pretty full-time job.

"What are you doing here?" I somehow managed to sound nonchalant, even though it felt like there was a frog in my throat.

"I caught a double last night. I was just heading home when I heard the call come in. And then I saw Rosemarie's car and my Spidey-sense started tingling."

"It could've been anyone's car," I said. "I'm sure dozens of people drive yellow Beetles in this city."

I could practically feel his shrug. "Perhaps. But not all of them decorate the headlights with big eyelashes or have vanity plates that say HT4TCHR."

I couldn't argue with that. Rosemarie wasn't known for her subtlety.

"So what's the situation?" he asked.

I was being an idiot. I couldn't keep hiding behind the car door and not face him. I was a grown woman. And my legs had fallen asleep.

"We were just passing by," I said, hoisting myself out of the crouch I was in. I bit my lip to keep from whimpering and half dragged myself back into the passenger seat, rubbing the stinging needles out of my legs. "Just another day in the life of me. Several shots were fired and it turns out my Aunt Scarlet is inside."

"Is she the one who was in the OSS and killed all her husbands?" he asked.

"Yes to the OSS," I said. "She probably didn't kill her husbands. At least on purpose. Probably being married to her is enough to kill any man."

"The women in your family are hell on men," Nick said.

That was pretty much the truth. Scarlet had outlived five husbands, my mother had outlived my father, and my sister Phoebe chewed men up and spit them out on a regular basis. And come to think of it, I wasn't doing so hot either. I'd never been married, but I'd accidentally hit my ex-fiancé with my car. It turned out he'd been poisoned before he ran in front of me, so technically I didn't kill him.

I finally looked up and wished I hadn't. Nick looked terrible. His face was gaunt, and a couple days growth of beard covered his face. His slacks and dress shirt were wrinkled and he'd taken his tie off somewhere along the way, so his collar was open and his undershirt peeked through. He hadn't even bothered with a coat, though it was almost freezing outside and little puffs of white fog escaped his mouth. His hair was a little longer since I'd last seen him, but he worked so much there was never time to get it cut. His expression was grim. The double he'd caught must've been a bad one.

"You okay?" I asked.

"I've been better. You ever meet Rick Chandler? He was a sergeant out of patrol."

"Never heard of him." And then I caught on. "*Was*?"

Nick's eyes went cold as ice and he nodded. "A neighbor heard shots and called 9-1-1. At first glance it looks like a murder/suicide. Chandler and his wife have been on the rocks for more than a year now. He had a girlfriend and the wife wasn't too happy about it."

"I can imagine," I said, brows raised. "Wives are weird like that. So she offed him and turned the gun on herself?"

"Nope, other way around. Only problem is, Chandler was a lefty. And though we train to shoot with both hands, Chandler could only shoot with his left, because he broke most of the bones in his right hand about a decade ago. His trigger finger didn't bend. Guess which hand the gun was found in?"

"I'm going to go with the right."

"There you have it," he said. "We're looking hard, but nothing has come up so far. I figured an armed robbery at the gas station might clear my mind."

"Something only a cop would say."

"I'm starting to think it might have been a rash decision. I've never seen your Aunt Scarlet, but am I right to presume she's the one in the fur coat facing off with the gunman like Dirty Harry?"

I sighed. "Yep, that's her. She's supposed to be on a single's cruise in Italy, so I'm not sure what she's still doing in Savannah."

I was trying to act cool, but in truth my stomach was in knots and a ball of fear was lodged in my throat. Despite her eccentricities, I loved Scarlet. I wanted to be just like her when I was ninety. I was pretty good at holding things together during a crisis. I'd really never had a choice in my family. Between my mother and my sister, there was enough drama to go around, and I was always the one left to be the responsible adult. Which was terrifying if you thought about it. I was thirty years old—thirty-one in another week—and just starting to get my shit together.

"Are you doing okay?" Nick asked. "You look a little pale."

"I'm good. The gunshots worried me a bit, but Scarlet is still standing. She's actually got a musket ball lodged in her hip. One of her husbands collected antique weapons and it misfired. Though Scarlet likes to tell everyone he shot her on purpose."

"She seems like a handful," Nick said. "Must run in the family. By the way, does your Aunt Scarlet carry a big silver revolver in her purse?" Nick squinted. "Looks like a .44."

Rosemarie and I both shot up to a standing position and watched in horror as Scarlet held the revolver in a two-handed grip, right at the robber's mid-section. They were in a standoff, and I figured the gun weighed almost as much as Scarlet. I watched in fascination as the expression on the robber's face changed and he started shaking his head. I couldn't hear what she was saying, but I didn't have to, to know that Scarlet was reading him the riot act. She was mean as a snake when she wanted to be.

The robber backed up a few steps, but didn't lower his gun. That was his mistake. The *crack* from the revolver made me flinch and I heard gasps—including my own—as she fired point blank at the robber. The only problem was, the revolver kicked like a mule and the recoil adjusted her aim upward several inches. The gun thwacked her in the head and Scarlet went down for the count.

A high-pitched scream was heard from inside and the robber came running out, one hand holding up the gun in surrender and the other pressed against his ear.

"Crazy bitch!" he yelled, his voice a couple octaves higher than normal. "Fuckin' bitch shot my ear off. What the hell is the wrong with the old people in this city?"

Police cars had swarmed in around us and they all held their weapons on the robber, demanding he get down on the ground, while he danced around in pain.

Hostages started filing out the front door, looking a little dazed, but there was no Scarlet, so I started toward the door. Despite the fact that she always seemed larger than life and scary as hell, she was still a ninety-year-old woman.

But before I could get there Scarlet stumbled out the front door, her giant handbag hanging over one arm, the other wrapped around a very attractive man who was at least fifty years younger than she was. There was a knot the size of a goose egg right in the middle of her forehead, and bruising was already forming around her eyes, making her look like a raccoon. The gun was nowhere in sight. Probably for the best.

"You're going to need another box of donuts," Nick said. "She looks like she could use a few."

"It feels a little weird standing and talking like this. Like everything is normal."

"Everything *is* normal. I love you and you love me. You're just being a stubborn dummy. And stop avoiding me. It's not like I'm going to re-ask you to marry me every time we're in the general vicinity. I've missed seeing you."

I sighed as that clawing feel of panic started rising up inside me, just like it had the first time I'd been left at the altar. And then a wave of sadness washed over me. "I've missed seeing you too," I finally said. "A lot."

"That makes me feel better," Nick said, grinning for the first time that morning. "Serves you right. Clock's ticking, Addison. Your month is almost over. You're going to have to give me an answer soon."

My eyes narrowed and my hands went to my hips. "I know what damned day it is," I said.

"Good, because the second your time is up I'm taking the tracker off my car. I can promise you won't see me coming."

He grasped hold of my arms and pulled me into him for a hard, fast kiss. I might have melted against him a little too long. It was hard to be sure because he'd scrambled my neurons, and I was wishing desperately I'd taken the time to put on underwear that morning.

I vaguely heard Aunt Scarlet somewhere in the background telling her rescuer she wanted him to meet her niece. I assumed she was talking about me, and I rolled my eyes before I could help it.

Nick grinned and let me go. "See you around," he said, whistling as he headed back to his truck.

"Maybe I need to forget about looking for men at assisted living," Rosemarie said. "Maybe I should hang out at the police station more."

"Statistically, cops don't make the best husbands," I said, frowning. Though I knew several who'd been able to make it work.

"That's okay. I'm thinking I might still be in the rebound stage before I find *the one*. I hear cops are excellent rebounders. Plus, they carry all kinds of interesting things on their belts. Like handcuffs and those little leather paddles."

"The only cops that carry little leather paddles are the ones at Chippendales. Real cops aren't into spanking while making an arrest."

"That's a shame," she said. "Seems like it would make things more interesting."

ABOUT THE AUTHOR

Liliana Hart is a *New York Times*, *USA Today*, and Publisher's Weekly bestselling author of more than sixty titles. After starting her first novel her freshman year of college, she immediately became addicted to writing and knew she'd found what she was meant to do with her life. She has no idea why she majored in music.

Since publishing in June 2011, Liliana has sold more than six-million books. All three of her series have made multiple appearances on the New York Times list.

Liliana can almost always be found at her computer writing, hauling five kids to various activities, or spending time with her husband. She calls Texas home.

If you enjoyed reading *this*, I would appreciate it if you would help others enjoy this book, too.

 Lend it. This e-book is lending-enabled, so please, share it with a friend.

Recommend it. Please help other readers find this book by recommending it to friends, readers' groups and discussion boards.

Review it. Please tell other readers why you liked this book by reviewing.

Connect with me online:
www.lilianahart.com

facebook.com/LilianaHart

twitter.com/Liliana_Hart

instagram.com/LilianaHart

bookbub.com/authors/liliana-hart

ALSO BY LILIANA HART

Addison Holmes Mystery Series

Whiskey Rebellion

Whiskey Sour

Whiskey For Breakfast

Whiskey, You're The Devil

Whiskey on the Rocks

Whiskey Tango Foxtrot

Whiskey and Gunpowder

JJ Graves Mystery Series

Dirty Little Secrets

A Dirty Shame

Dirty Rotten Scoundrel

Down and Dirty

Dirty Deeds

Dirty Laundry

Dirty Money

A Dirty Job

Books by Liliana Hart and Scott Silverii

The Harley and Davidson Mystery Series

The Farmer's Slaughter

A Tisket a Casket

I Saw Mommy Killing Santa Claus

Get Your Murder Running

Deceased and Desist

Malice In Wonderland

Tequila Mockingbird

Gone With the Sin

The MacKenzies of Montana

Dane's Return

Thomas's Vow

Riley's Sanctuary

Cooper's Promise

Grant's Christmas Wish

The MacKenzies Boxset

MacKenzie Security Series

Seduction and Sapphires

Shadows and Silk

Secrets and Satin

Sins and Scarlet Lace

Sizzle

Crave

Trouble Maker

Scorch

MacKenzie Security Omnibus 1

MacKenzie Security Omnibus 2

The Gravediggers

The Darkest Corner

Gone to Dust

Say No More

Lawmen of Surrender (MacKenzies-1001 Dark Nights)

1001 Dark Nights: Captured in Surrender

1001 Dark Nights: The Promise of Surrender

Sweet Surrender

Dawn of Surrender

The MacKenzie World (read in any order)

Trouble Maker

Bullet Proof

Deep Trouble

Delta Rescue

Desire and Ice

Rush

Spies and Stilettos

Wicked Hot

Hot Witness

Avenged

Never Surrender

Stand Alone Titles

Breath of Fire

Kill Shot

Catch Me If You Can

All About Eve

Paradise Disguised

Island Home

The Witching Hour

Made in the USA
Monee, IL
13 August 2021